W9-CEU-334

VALLEY COTTAGE FREE LIBRARY

3 2641 01029 4410

October 2018

Valley Cottage Library
110 Route 303
Valley Cottage, NY
10989

www.vclib.org

Bah! Humbug!

Bah! Humbug!

Michael Rosen

Illustrated by

Tony Ross

WALKER BOOKS

Chapter 1

"Your Scrooge mask?" Ray Gruber yelled as the family climbed into the car. "Your Scrooge mask, Harry? I have no idea where it is. I'm just guessing . . ." He switched to his sarcastic voice. "Let me see . . . I wonder, just wonder, if it's . . . *exactly where you left it?*"

Harry Gruber felt himself shrink under his father's words. He had only been allowed to bring the mask home because he had pleaded with Miss

Cavani to have it overnight so he could practice some Scrooge expressions in the mirror. He loved seeing himself turn from somebody no one noticed, an eleven-year-old guy with cheeks that were really annoying, he thought (too wide one day, too long the next), into a mean, crabby, whiny old man whom hundreds of people would be staring at in a show — all done with what his drama teacher called a half-mask. It covered his forehead, eyes, and most of those annoying cheeks and gave him a new, narrow, slightly twisted nose. And yet underneath that was his own mouth: somehow looking like a new, not-his-own, very old mouth. How amazing was that? In front of the mirror he had practiced sneering, cackling, bullying, being shocked, being afraid, being regretful . . .

What you feel, Harry, we feel, Miss Cavani had said, *but we have to see it, dear, see it in your face and in your shoulders.* That was a challenge. How do you show how you feel in your shoulders?

But now — oh, rats! He had left the mask back in the house, somewhere no-idea-where, and this had annoyed Dad. Again. *Why am I so good at annoying Dad?* Harry wondered. He looked up at the street-lamp throwing its light on them. *Wouldn't it be great if every time you felt bad, you could turn yourself into a thing?* Like the streetlamp. Being useful and never feeling bad. Just standing there throwing light on this street of town houses.

Dad's voice interrupted his thoughts: "And I'm not going to ask why, in the name of the stars above, your school thought it was a good idea to do A *Christmas* crummy *Carol* on the night before Christmas. If they were going to do anything on the night before Christmas, it should have been 'The Night Before crummy Christmas.' Ha!"

Harry hadn't waited to hear the whole speech and had scuttled back into the house to hunt down the mask. His mom had switched off the lights as they were leaving, so now he had a touch of heart-hopping as his own shadow, cast by the street-lamp reaching into the house through the window, chased him up the stairs.

"Ray," said Harry's mother, Lisa, in the most

soothing voice she could conjure up, but it came out as a voice that sounded angry that she had to try and make soothing. She glanced at herself in the mirror on the back of the car's visor and moved a lock of hair onto her forehead.

"I'm ready," said Ray, sitting down heavily in the driver's seat.

"We can't go, Ray, until Harry's got his Scrooge mask. So we're not 'ready,' are we?"

There was a lot of weight in the "ready."

Ray started the car.

"And my chair's not in," chipped in Eva, Harry's younger sister.

"What?" Lisa exclaimed. She was shocked.

Ray furiously untangled himself from his seat belt, muttering curses and excuses to himself or to the car or to the gatepost or to the chair itself, all to the effect that if Harry hadn't stuck his Scrooge mask in some deep dark recess of the house, he, Ray, wouldn't have forgotten to put Eva's chair in the car.

"I don't even know why we all have to go, any-way . . ." He went on digging in his own irritated groove as he deftly heaved the chair into the back of the car.

Lisa turned from soothing to not-soothing. "I'm going to see our son doing his very best at something. That's all. I thought you'd want to do that too." Her voice crackled through the open windows of the car, as frosty as the frost that was crouching, ready to pounce at that moment in the middle of the night when the street would turn out its lights and fall asleep.

Eva agreed. "I want to see Harry do Scrooge. He's shown me tons of it already."

Lisa said, "Oh, well, if he flubs his lines, you can call them out."

Eva giggled. "He'd never forgive me."

Ray got himself behind the wheel again. His tone changed, dropping the irritation and sarcastic whine, as he said, "I want to see this thing too, I do, but look. You know and I know if we had gotten this material up online over Christmas, the site would increase its traffic by—what?—ten percent? Twenty percent? But that's fine, I'm coming . . ."

Then the old sarcasm cut in again: "If my family thinks it can wait, it can wait-widdly-wait."

"You always say that," Eva said quietly, spotting the change in Dad's tone.

But Ray was working himself up, and nothing was going to stop him now, not even Eva. "Hello? Hello? Can anyone hear me? I'm talking about what pays for all this." He waved in the general direction of everything.

The family knew all about Ray's "everything." When he waved his "everything" hand in the air, it could mean the egg they were having for breakfast, the TV, the car, the hoodie that Harry would die for, the beach vacation they took in August, the local neighborhood's offerings of such delights as a Greek diner and a fifties replica ice-cream parlor, or the whole world—all of it. And they all had to be grateful.

Harry loomed up beside the car. He had the Scrooge mask in his hand. His face looked panicked.

Ray slumped forward over the wheel, his jacket stretched like a sausage skin over his shoulders.

"It's broken," Harry whimpered. "I must have . . . have . . . er . . ."

"Get in," Lisa said, using the soothing voice again. "The most important thing is being on time for the show. The mask comes second. Drive, Ray."

Eva looked at the mask. Though she could see the break, she said, "It's not too bad, Harry. No one will notice."

Harry groaned. Sometimes, Mom and Eva being so darned nice and helpful was nearly as bad as Dad being sarcastic.

Ray eased into gear.

"But . . ." Harry looked at the mask with despair.

Lisa flicked her fingers. Harry passed it to her. She ran an expert hand over the cracked part just below the eye, dug around in her bag, pulled out some robust-looking white tape, and, as the car headed off and down the road, with the headlights pouring over the newsstand on the left, the barber's and the drugstore on the right, she neatly stuck it together.

Eva looked sideways at her mom; their faces lit then darkened as the car shot past the street-lamps. The white tape that solves everything! Eva remembered how proud she had been when, at school, they were talking about the jobs their parents did, and she had said, "My mom's an assistant director — she tells actors where to stand and sticks bits of tape on the floor to mark where their feet go."

Lisa tucked the roll of tape back in her bag.

In truth, Harry wasn't as late as the Ghost of Christmas Past, who said he was late because he had to come all the way from the Past to the Present.

No one laughed at that, least of all Harry, who was by now nervous *times four*. He was nervous because he was worried about his lines, nervous about whether he was any good at saying the lines, nervous about whether his mask would fall apart, nervous about whether . . . about whether Dad would think it was worth coming. On the way home later, would Dad talk on and on and on about how the show wasn't all that good and how it would have been better if he had done some work . . . ?

The pre-show chatter was building to the level of a playground after a pop quiz: mascara wands were passing from hand to hand; umbrellas, Victorian shawls, top hats, and pewter mugs were being gripped and twisted. The "street sellers" (Rory, Sunil, Crayton, Rasheda, Stefan, and Désol'é) were pitching their laughter up to the level of cheerleaders stirring up a crowd.

Even in the midst of his nerves, Harry knew he loved this excitement. Stefan and Désol'é looked like they had a thing going, but everyone had been saying that for months now. Rasheda, serious Rasheda, who was always the first to stop anyone from goofing around in class, had turned into some kind of fireball; the show seemed to have made her just slightly crazy, Harry thought. Miss Cavani had recruited Rory, Sunil, and Crayton from the basketball team. She had barged into the Monday-night practice, announcing that she needed three kids who could move and shout. "That's what you, you, and you have been doing for the last five minutes. Perfect!" There was something about the way Miss Cavani said things that made everyone do what she asked. Off went the floppy jerseys with the big numbers on the back, on went the black Victorian gear. But they were still being all slam dunk and high fives right now. Harry smiled to himself behind his mask.

Miss Cavani clapped her hands. "Breathing. Remember? In—and one and two and three and four. Out—and one and two and three and four."

As she breathed in, her eyes gleamed and her chest expanded. The laughter and hugging subsided. Through the door of the offstage classroom G29, which Miss Cavani insisted on calling the "Green Room," she caught sight of Harry, peeking at the audience.

"Come away from the curtain, Harry. They'll see

your eye staring out at them, kiddo. We want them to be scared by the show, not by your eyeball."

A snicker snaked through the cast. The now-quiet street sellers silently reassured each other with touched fists. Harry ducked back in. He loved being chewed out by Miss Cavani.

He had spotted Mom, Dad, and Eva. It had been easy: Dad had his cell phone on, and the light lit up the frown on his face.

Dickens: Marley was dead. There is no doubt whatever about that. Old Marley was as dead as a doornail.

Mind! I don't know what's particularly dead about a doornail.

Scrooge: Marley and I were partners for I don't know how many years. I was his sole friend, and sole mourner at the funeral. I never painted out Old Marley's name. There the

11

firm's name stood, years afterward, above the warehouse door: Scrooge and Marley. Sometimes people new to the business called me Scrooge, and sometimes Marley, but I answered to both names. It was all the same to me.

Dickens: Oh! But he was a tight-fisted hand at the grindstone, Scrooge! A squeezing, wrenching, grasping, scraping, clutching, covetous old sinner! And solitary as an oyster. The cold within him froze his old features, nipped his pointed nose, shriveled his cheek, stiffened his gait; made his eyes red and his thin lips blue. He carried his own low temperature always about with him; he iced his office and didn't thaw it one degree at Christmas.

Nobody ever stopped him in the street to say, "My dear Scrooge, how are you? When

will you come to see me?" No beggars implored him to bestow a trifle, no children asked him what it was o'clock, no man or woman ever once in all his life inquired the way to such and such a place, of Scrooge. But what did Scrooge care!

Scrooge: That's how I liked it.

Miss Cavani had warned Harry that there would be times when the audience would hiss at him.

"They won't be hissing at you, Harry. They'll be hissing at Scrooge," she had reassured him.

Sure enough, they hissed.

Harry stared back at them. He caught sight of his father, his head attached to his phone. Harry's stare turned into contempt, which brought on yet more hissing.

Dickens: Once upon a time — of all the good days in the year, on Christmas Eve — old Scrooge sat busy in his countinghouse.

Scrooge: It was cold, biting weather, and I could hear the people outside, wheezing up and down, beating their hands upon their breasts, and stamping their feet upon the pavement stones to warm them.

Dickens: The city clocks had only just gone three, but it was quite dark already. The dense fog came pouring in at every chink and keyhole. The door of Scrooge's counting-house office was open . . .

Scrooge: . . . so that I could peek through the door to keep my eye upon my clerk . . .

Dickens: . . . who, in a dismal little cell beyond, was copying letters. Scrooge had a very small fire, but the clerk's fire was so very much smaller that it looked like one coal. Which is why the clerk put on his white scarf and tried to warm himself at the candle; in which effort, not being a man of a strong imagination, he failed.

Scrooge's Nephew: A Merry Christmas, Uncle! God save you!

Scrooge: Bah! Humbug!

Back came a loud booing. Harry wasn't ready for that. For a split second, it annoyed him. Without knowing why, he threw back at them a second:

Scrooge: Humbug!!

He sensed that Shona, playing Dickens, was caught offbeat with her next line, but she took another breath and came in with the little insert that Miss Cavani had written for, as she said, "your younger brothers and sisters."

Dickens: What is this "humbug"? I'm famous for putting this in this story, but people have sometimes mistaken it for a sweet, a hard-boiled minty sweet. No, no, no, "humbug" means "false," or as you might say, "bogus" or "phony."

Harry glanced at Eva as Shona spoke. He wanted Eva to like Shona. He wanted Eva to like it that he liked Shona.

Nephew: Christmas a humbug, Uncle! You don't mean that, I'm sure.

Scrooge: I do. Merry Christmas! What right have you

to be merry? What reason have you to be merry? You're poor enough.

Nephew: Come, then. What right have you to be dismal? What reason have you to be morose? You're rich enough.

Scrooge: Bah! Humbug.

Nephew: Don't be cross, Uncle.

Scrooge: What else can I be, when I live in such a world of fools out upon Merry Christmas! What's Christmastime to you but a time for finding yourself a year older, but not an hour richer? If I could work my will, every idiot who goes about with "Merry Christmas" on his lips should be boiled with his own pudding and buried with a stake of holly through his heart. He should!

Nephew: Uncle!

Scrooge: Nephew! Keep Christmas in your own way, and let me keep it in mine.

Nephew: Keep it? But you don't keep it.

Scrooge: Let me leave it alone, then. Much good may it do you! Much good it has ever done you!

Nephew: I am sure I have always thought of Christmastime, when it has come round, as a kind, forgiving, charitable, pleasant time: the only time I know of, in the long calendar of the year, when men and women seem to open their shut-up hearts and to think of people below them as if they really were fellow passengers to the grave. And therefore, Uncle, though it has never put a scrap of gold or silver in my pocket, I believe that it *has* done me good, and *will* do me good; and I say, God bless it!

Dickens: The clerk applauded. Becoming

immediately aware that he shouldn't have, he poked the fire and extinguished the last frail spark forever.

Scrooge (*to the clerk*): Let me hear another sound from you, and you'll keep your Christmas by losing your job.

Scrooge (*to his nephew*): You're quite a powerful speaker, sir, I wonder you don't go into Parliament.

Nephew: Don't be angry, Uncle. Come! Dine with us tomorrow.

Scrooge: I would rather see you in hell.

Nephew: But why? I want nothing from you; I ask nothing of you; why cannot we be friends?

Scrooge: Good afternoon.

Nephew: I am sorry, with all my heart, to find you so stubborn. We have never had any quarrel, and I'll keep my Christmas humor to the last. So a Merry Christmas, Uncle!

Scrooge: Good afternoon!

Nephew: And a Happy New Year!

Scrooge: Good afternoon!

Dickens: His nephew left the room without an angry word.

Nephew: Merry Christmas, Mr. Cratchit.

Bob Cratchit: Merry Christmas to you, too.

Scrooge (*muttering*): There's another fellow, Bob Cratchit, my clerk, with fifteen shillings a week, and a wife and family, talking about a "Merry Christmas." I'll retire to the madhouse.

Ray mouthed silently to Lisa.

Lisa didn't understand. Or pretended not to understand. She was gripped by the show and had already felt teary several times seeing how well Harry was doing. Now Ray was mouthing at her.

Ray insisted, saw he was getting nowhere, and then whispered in Lisa's ear, "I've got to go in. This is big. Mumbai."

Lisa turned to look at the man she thought loved her and their family more than anything in the world. And here he was, whispering in her ear—

not "Isn't Harry doing great," not "I'm glad you made me come to the show," not "I love you, Lisa," but instead whispering "Mumbai." She didn't even know why he was whispering "Mumbai." Worse: it infuriated her that he was whispering "Mumbai."

His eyes were full of passion. He leaned into her ear once more: "Ka-ching!" he whispered with a little squeal at the end. It was his moneymaking sound he loved to make. Ray started to lift his backside off the chair.

Lisa put her hand on Ray's leg and pressed down.

Dickens: In letting Scrooge's nephew out, Bob Cratchit let two other people in. They were portly gentlemen, pleasant to look at, and now stood, with their hats off, in Scrooge's office.

Gentleman: Scrooge and Marley's, I believe. Have I the pleasure of addressing Mr. Scrooge or Mr. Marley?

Scrooge: Mr. Marley died seven years ago this very night.

Gentleman (*taking up his pen*): At this festive season of the year, Mr. Scrooge, it is more than usually desirable that we should make some slight provision for the poor and destitute, who suffer greatly at the present time. Many thousands are in want of everyday things; hundreds of thousands are in need of comfort, sir.

Scrooge: Are there no prisons?

Gentleman: Plenty of prisons.

Scrooge: And the workhouses? Are they still in operation?

Gentleman: They are. Still, I wish I could say they were not.

Scrooge: The Treadmill and the Poor Law are still in fine shape, then?

Gentleman: Both very busy, sir.

Scrooge: Oh! I was afraid, from what you said at first, that something had occurred to stop them in their useful course. I'm very glad to hear it.

Gentleman: A few of us are trying to raise a fund to buy the poor some meat and drink, and means of warmth. We choose this time, because it is a time, of all others, when want is keenly felt, and abundance is shared. What shall I put you down for?

Scrooge: Nothing!

Gentleman: You wish to be anonymous?

Scrooge: I wish to be left alone. Since you ask me what I wish, gentlemen, that is my answer. I don't make merry myself at Christmas and I can't afford to make idle people merry. I help to support the establishments I have mentioned — they cost enough and those who are badly off must go there.

Gentleman: Many can't go there, and many would rather die.

Scrooge: If they would rather die, they had better do it, and decrease the surplus population. Good afternoon, gentlemen!

Dickens: And the gentlemen saw themselves out.

Harry had always liked it that Scrooge's bitter words had the power to send the gentlemen away. *No booing or hissing this time,* he thought as his eyes wandered over the audience again. Then, just as he felt a tremor of pleasure pass down his back, his eyes reached Dad. He could see him pull himself away from Mom's arm and Eva's glare and leave. Deep in Harry's stomach, something started grinding. It was a slow, dull heaviness.

Dickens: At length the hour of shutting up the countinghouse arrived. With an ill will, Scrooge dismounted from his stool. Bob Cratchit instantly snuffed his candle out and put on his hat.

Scrooge: You'll want all day tomorrow off, I suppose?

Bob: If that'd be convenient, sir.

Scrooge: It's not convenient, and it's not fair. If I was to dock you half a crown for it, you'd think yourself hard done by, I'll be bound? And yet, you don't think *me* hard done by when I pay you a day's wages for doing no work.

Bob: It is only once a year, sir.

Scrooge: A poor excuse for picking a man's pocket every twenty-fifth of December! But I suppose you must have the whole day. Be here all the earlier next morning!

Bob: Yes, sir!

Dickens: Scrooge walked out with a growl. The office was closed in a twinkling, and the clerk, with the long ends of his white scarf dangling below his waist — he had no coat — ran home to his family in Camden Town as fast as he could. Scrooge took his melancholy dinner in his usual melancholy tavern; and having read all the newspapers, and whiled away the rest of the evening with his banker's book, went home.

Ray sprinted to the car. *Mumbai!* If they could clinch this one tonight, it would change everything. GruberMeister.com would be global. *Global Gruber!*

He slammed the car door shut. *What Lisa doesn't get is that global doesn't just mean global. It means time. Global time. Twenty-four-hour days. It's not just that Mumbai is here. Mumbai is now.*

He whirled the steering wheel around with a little flourish, and the car purred toward the school gates. He tapped the wheel as he waited for them to open automatically and glanced to his right at the booth where Malik the security guy usually sat on nights like this.

Hmph, no one here tonight . . . that's odd.

Ray's eyes switched back to watch the gates creak open and then whipped back to the booth.

Sitting still and smiling in the booth was Kwame. *Kwame?!* His best friend from school. They had even gone to the same college! The hours they spent, their heads full of dreams of how they could change the world: desalinate the sea and get fresh water to places that hadn't seen rain for years, use recycled trucks and containers to house the homeless . . . and then . . . Oh, hell and hell and hell again, why was it that dear Kwame had parked on the shoulder of the highway, opened the hood of his old car, and, as a jet of screaming hot steam hit his face, staggered out into traffic and been killed instantly?

Ray stared at Kwame.

Kwame smiled back.

Ray heard himself gasp. He looked at the gates still creeping open as if Kwame were controlling them. Yet again, Ray looked back at Kwame, but he was gone. No one was there. Nothing. Just the empty booth, with a picture of the school team stuck slightly crookedly on the back wall. Ray heard a step next to the car. A face loomed up into the window. It was Malik.

"Merry Christmas, Mr. Gruber," he said.

"Yes, yes," Ray muttered back, and pulled out of the parking lot as fast as he could. *Better not to assume that was actually Malik,* he thought.

Grubermeister operated from an office unit in an industrial park on a long, winding, unlit exit off the highway. As Ray drove the car along this road, he switched the headlights to high beams, but the dark crowded in on the shaft of light. He slowed down. There was something strange about the darkness tonight, something heavy, almost as if it had gathered around the car like a cloth, and it was the cloth that was slowing the car down and not him. He couldn't stop himself from staring out into it. Into his mind came the picture of poor dear Kwame staggering out into the road — not something he had seen but had only imagined as the news had filtered through about how he had died.

Scrooge: Now, it is a fact that there was nothing at all particular about the knocker on my door, except that it was very large. It is also a fact, that I had seen it, night and morning, during the whole time I lived in that place. And then let any man explain to me, if he can, how it happened that I, having my key in the lock of the door, saw not a knocker, but Marley's face!

Dickens: Marley's face. It had a dismal light about it, like a bad lobster in a dark cellar. It was not angry or ferocious, but looked at Scrooge as Marley used to look. The hair was curiously stirred, as if by breath or hot air; and, though the eyes were wide open, they were perfectly motionless. That, and its livid color, made it horrible.

Scrooge: But then, suddenly, it was a knocker again. To say that I was not startled would be untrue. But I put my hand upon the key I had let go of, turned it sturdily, walked in, and lighted my candle.

Dickens: He *did* pause, before he shut the door, and he *did* look cautiously behind the door first, as if he half expected to be terrified with the sight of Marley's hair tied into a pigtail sticking out into the hall.

Scrooge: Nothing on the back of the door, except the screws and nuts that hold the knocker on.

Dickens: Up the stairs Scrooge went, trimming his candle and not caring a button for the darkness; darkness is cheap. But before he shut his heavy door, Scrooge walked through his rooms to see that all was right.

Scrooge: Sitting room, bedroom, lumber room. All as they should be. Nobody under the table; nobody under the sofa; nobody under the bed; nobody in the closet; nobody in my dressing gown, hanging up in that suspicious way against the wall.

Dickens: Quite satisfied, he closed his door and locked himself in; double-locked himself in. Thus secured against surprise, Scrooge took off his cravat, put on his dressing gown and slippers, and his nightcap, and sat down before the fire to take his gruel.

Scrooge: Humbug!

Dickens: Scrooge threw his head back in the chair, and his glance happened to rest upon a disused bell that hung in the room. It was with great astonishment, and with a strange dread, he saw this bell begin to swing. It swung so softly in the outset that it scarcely made a sound; but soon it rang out loudly, and so did every bell in the house.

"How are you going to make the bell swing all on its own?" Eva had asked Harry one time when he was rehearsing. Harry wasn't going to give anything away. He just tapped the side of his nose. Well, not his nose, actually. The mask's nose.

When the bell moved in the show itself, Eva remembered this chat. And still she couldn't see what made the bell move. She pointed at it, as if Mom might not have seen it. She mimed it moving with her hands. Lisa smiled and shrugged as if to say, *How do I know?*

But Eva knew that Mom would know exactly how and smiled. Anyone who sticks tape on the floor to tell actors where to stand would know how to make a bell move all on its own. *Maybe, one day, I could do that too,* she thought. *No. Maybe I could be like that Shona, who Harry seems to like so much, and it would be me making sure I was in the right place where the tape was stuck down . . .*

The units in the industrial park crouched in the darkness. Even Unit 9B, Grubermeister, was dark, as the windows were in the roof and on the other side.

The team liked the futuristic anonymity of the plain gray front wall of the unit. It could almost be a UFO and they were anywhere, nowhere and everywhere.

Ray passed the electronic fob over the pad, and the door slid open. He stepped in, and the door closed automatically. At the end of the hall, he could see a line of light at the base of the door. He walked toward it, and for a moment wondered if, when he opened it, Kwame would be sitting waiting for him.

Dickens: The bells were followed by a clanking noise, deep down below, as if some person were dragging a heavy chain in the cellar.

Scrooge: Ghosts! Don't they say ghosts in haunted houses can be heard dragging chains?

Dickens: There was a booming sound, of the cellar door flying open, and then he heard the noise much louder, on the floors below, then coming up the stairs; then coming straight toward his door.

Scrooge: It's humbug still! I won't believe it.

Dickens: His color changed though, when, without a pause, it came on through the heavy door, and passed into the room before his eyes.

Scrooge: The same face: the very same. Marley!

Ray passed the fob over the pad, and the door opened inward. It wasn't Kwame; it was François. He had two monitors up and a laptop in front of them and was glancing between all three screens. The low purr of the keys crept out of his fingertips.

Without looking up, François calmly greeted Ray in his half-American, half-French accent: "This is unnecessary."

"What is?"

"You."

Ray laughed.

"I'm serious," François said, his eyes never leaving the screens.

"*Vraiment?*" Ray prodded back. "Really?"

François swung around on his chair and looked up at Ray. "You know how we do that thing on Monday mornings?"

"Hmm?" Ray didn't know where this was going. He had a sense that tonight was turning into a night of not knowing where things were going.

"Prioritize Time. PT! What are your priorities tonight, Ray?"

"Oh, shut up, will you!" Ray snapped back. "You texted me. I didn't text you."

"I was passing the informations on to you, Ray. You say that's what makes us strong. We share always the informations. Your job now is with the Grubers, not with Grubermeister."

"No, it's you who's got this wrong, François." Ray poked his finger at him. "Grubermeister is what keeps the Grubers floating on the river and—"

François interrupted: "Is Harry doing the show tonight?"

Ray nodded.

François said nothing. He just nodded back in a heavy, significant way.

Ray got the point. "There'll be other shows. And yet more shows. How many nativity plays do I have to see?"

"*Christmas Carol* is a nativity play?"

"No, no, no. You know what I mean . . ." Ray's eyes moved to the screens. He took it all in with a glance.

François lifted his hand up between them. "When my family moved to Bordeaux, you know, it was because my mother had the job in the city. My father stayed on the land."

Ray pretended to ignore this and tapped a few keys. The screens wiped and flashed.

"I went to see him before I moved to California."

"Look at this!" Ray's voice rose.

"We talked about sheep and chickens," François carried on calmly. "As I left, we embraced, you know, *en famille*—we kiss on both sides, four times in all! He gave me the hug and said very quiet, 'So sorry, Frou.' It's what he called me. Frou is a rabbit—no, a hare—in a story we have in France."

Ray could hear that François's voice had become unsteady. He knew, without looking, François's eyes were wet.

"Papa had missed it all. I was the four-hundred-meter youth champion in Bordeaux. Athletics."

Still without looking at him, Ray said quietly but fiercely, pointing his finger toward the screen, "This is what I'm doing. I'm doing it now. That's my decision. I know what I'm doing, and I know why I'm doing it. The last thing I need is someone dumping his family issues all over me."

There was total silence in the office except for the low hum of the computers.

Dickens: The chain Marley clasped about his middle. His body was transparent; Scrooge looked the phantom through

41

and through, and saw it standing before him; though he felt the chilling influence of its death-cold eyes; he was still incredulous, and fought against his senses.

Scrooge: How now! What do you want with me?

Ghost of Marley: Much!

Scrooge: Who are you?

Ghost: Ask me who I *was*.

Scrooge: Who *were* you, then?

Ghost: In life I was your partner, Jacob Marley. (*Pause.*) You don't believe in me.

Scrooge: I don't.

Ghost: Why do you doubt your senses?

Scrooge: Because, any little thing affects them. A slight disorder of the stomach makes them cheat. You may be an undigested bit of beef, a blot of mustard, a crumb of cheese, a fragment of an underdone potato. There's more of gravy than of grave about you, whatever you are!

Eva giggled. It was a high, birdlike giggle. The way Harry—(*My Harry,* she thought)—said "gravy" and "grave" seemed almost like a tickle. When Harry was rehearsing his words, she had to be all the other parts: Dickens, Marley—all of them. At first she had been shy and just said the lines in a very dull, flat way, but the more they rehearsed, the more she became the characters, the more she grew to love doing it.

There were times when Harry laughed at the way she did it. *He wasn't laughing at me,* Eva thought. *He was laughing with me because I was good at it.* And that had helped him.

Gravy . . . grave . . . she let the words go on tickling her.

Dickens: Scrooge was not much in the habit of cracking jokes. The truth is that he tried to be smart as a means of keeping down his terror, for the specter's voice disturbed the very marrow in his bones. Then the spirit raised a frightful cry, and shook its chain with such a dismal and appalling noise that Scrooge held on tight to his chair, to save himself from falling in a swoon.

Scrooge (*dropping to his knees*): Mercy! Dreadful apparition, why do you trouble me?

Ghost: Do you believe in me or not?

Scrooge: I do. I must. But why do spirits walk the earth, and why do they come to me?

Dickens: Again the specter raised a cry, and shook its chain, and wrung its shadowy hands.

Scrooge (*trembling*): You are fettered. Tell me why?

Ghost: I wear the chain I forged in life. I made it link by link, and yard by yard; I girded it on of my own free will, and of my own free will I wore it. Is its pattern strange to *you*?

Dickens: Scrooge trembled more and more.

Ghost: Or would you know the weight and length of the strong coil you bear yourself? It was full as heavy and as long as this, seven Christmas Eves ago. You have labored on it since. It is a ponderous chain!

Dickens: Scrooge glanced about him on the floor, in the expectation of finding himself surrounded by some fifty or sixty fathoms of iron cable, but he could see nothing.

46

What started off as a patter turned into a drumroll. Rain was hammering on the skylights above Ray's and François's heads. The weather had turned. High above them, clouds had rolled in, pushing the frost out. Now they were breaking into a downpour and creating electric charges across the sky. Lightning shot between the clouds, followed by thunder, while the rain hammered on.

Then the lights went out and the screens died.

Scrooge: Jacob, old Jacob Marley, tell me more. Speak comfort to me, Jacob.

Ghost: I have none to give. I cannot rest, I cannot stay, I cannot linger anywhere. My spirit never walked beyond our countinghouse — mark me! — in life my spirit never roved beyond the narrow limits of our money-changing hole; and weary journeys lie before me! Oh, captive, bound, and double-ironed. How was I to know that there is no amount of regret that can make up for life's opportunities misused! Yet such was I! Oh, such was I! At this time of the rolling year, I suffer most. Why did I walk through crowds of fellow beings with my eyes turned down, and never raise them to that blessed Star which led the Wise Men to a poor abode? Were there no poor homes to which its light would have conducted *me*!

Dickens: Scrooge began to quake exceedingly.

Ghost: Hear me! My time is nearly gone. I am here tonight to warn you, that you have yet a chance and hope of escaping my fate, Ebenezer.

Scrooge: You were always a good friend to me. Thank'ee!

Ghost: You will be haunted by Three Spirits.

Scrooge: Is that the chance and hope you mentioned,
            Jacob?

Ghost: It is.

Scrooge: I — I think I'd rather not.

Eva heard Mom's laugh next to her. Harry had made
Scrooge look so certain in his own nasty way, and
now, all of a sudden, he was like a little scared boy.
Eva stared at the stage. It was as if it wasn't Harry
anymore. He had become Scrooge. It really was
Scrooge who had said, "I think I'd rather not."

If Mom hadn't been there, Eva would have
called out, "Not so full of yourself now, are you,
Mr. Scrooge?"

Ghost: Without their visits, you cannot hope
            to shun the path I tread. Expect the first
            tomorrow, when the bell tolls one.

Scrooge: Couldn't I take 'em all at once, and have it over, Jacob?

Ghost: Expect the second on the next night at the same hour. The third upon the next night when the last stroke of twelve has ceased to vibrate. Look to see me no more; and look that, for your own sake, you remember what has passed between us.

Dickens: When it had said these words, the specter went to the window and floated out upon the bleak, dark night.

Chapter 2

Marvelous, marvelous! All of you!" Miss Cavani said in a loud whisper. "First Stave?" she asked, and everyone replied in silent mime, by making the victory sign with their parted fingers. "Shona, just watch that your mustache doesn't slip into your mouth, sweetheart. Come here, I can glue it down just a teeny bit more."

Miss Cavani attended to Shona. Harry wished he could attend to Shona instead. Stefan and Désol'é were doing mirror faces: one made a face and the other had to copy. It was one of Miss Cavani's exercises. The basketball trio were arguing in fierce whispers whether a three-point shot they had all seen in a game a few days earlier was after the buzzer or not.

Harry sat looking at his Scrooge shoes. They pinched his feet. That felt right. "Pinch" was one of the words he had written in his "Scrooge Journal" that Miss Cavani asked him to keep. The word sat alongside "One-track mind" and "Power." At the top of the page, he had written the question that Miss Cavani had fed him: *Is Scrooge content?* Content? Content? What does it even mean? "CON-tent" was one of Dad's words. "Online content," he would say. "I've got to head out and put up some more content," he had said in the middle of his cousin's wedding, Harry remembered, and slipped off to be with this "content."

He realized that as he was mulling over these

thoughts, he was staring at classroom G29's clock. During school, as it hit the hour, that evil buzzer would sound out across the whole building, but, thankfully, it was switched off after regular school hours. He imagined Dad, thinking of how long it would take him to get to the office, and he found himself wondering if Dad had always been like that.

Had he always been "there" rather than "here"? Content to be with his content?

Ray and François sat in the dark. For some reason the park's relay substation was vulnerable to electric storms.

"We're talking to Mumbai and we can't even get electricity from down the road into our unit," Ray muttered, hoping to make up with François with a bit of enjoyable grumbling.

"This is normal where my father lived in the countryside," François said, laughing. "Every summer, when I was a boy, always the escapes of water."

"Hm?"

"Coming through the roofs."

"Oh, yes, leaks," Ray added helpfully. It had worked. They were friends again. He continued talking: "Playing out late one time with my friend Stinker, there was one hell of a storm, and we stood under the big chestnut tree at the end of my road. At first, it was perfect. We looked up into the huge green umbrella above our heads, and we were so safe from the rain that we laughed. It wasn't because it was funny, though. We laughed . . . because . . . it was . . ."

"Nice?"

"Yeah . . . and then, this is the point . . . the

leaves started leaking! *Plop, plop, plop,* on the tops of our heads and on our noses . . . and we laughed even more. That's something. When you're a kid, you laugh at things even though they're not funny. I haven't thought of that before."

Dickens: When Scrooge awoke, the chimes of a neighboring church struck the four quarters. So he listened for the hour.

Scrooge: Six? Seven! Eight? Nine! Ten! Eleven! Twelve! Twelve? It was past two when I went to bed. The clock's wrong. An icicle must have got into the works. Twelve! (*Checks his pocket watch.*) Why, it isn't possible that I can have slept through a whole day and far into another night. It isn't possible that anything has happened to the sun, and this is twelve at noon!

Dickens: The idea being an alarming one, Scrooge

scrambled out of bed and groped his way to the window. He had to rub the frost off with the sleeve of his dressing gown before he could see anything, and could see very little then.

Scrooge: There is no noise of people running to and fro, and making a great stir, as there would be if night had beaten off bright day and taken possession of the world.

Dickens: Sighing with relief, Scrooge went to bed again, and thought, and thought, and thought it over and over, and could make nothing of it. The more he thought, the more perplexed he was; and the more he tried not to think, the more he thought of Marley's Ghost. Every time he resolved within himself that it was all a dream, his mind flew back, like a strong spring released, to its first position, and presented the same problem to be worked through:

Scrooge: Was it a dream or not?

Dickens: Scrooge lay in this state until the chime had gone three quarters more, when he remembered, all of a sudden, that the Ghost had warned him of a visitation when the bell tolled one. He promised himself to lie awake until the hour was past; and, considering that he could no more go to sleep than go to Heaven, this wasn't a difficult task.

(*Ding, dong!*)

Scrooge: A quarter past.

(*Ding, dong!*)

Half past!

(*Ding, dong!*)

A quarter to it.

(*Ding, dong!*)

The hour itself and nothing else!

Dickens: Scrooge spoke before the hour bell sounded, which it now did with a deep, dull, hollow, melancholy ONE. The curtains of his bed were drawn aside, and Scrooge found himself face-to-face with the unearthly visitor who drew them. It was a strange figure, like a child — yet not so like a child as like an old man, viewed through some supernatural medium. Its hair was white as if with age, and yet the face had not a wrinkle in it. The arms were very long and muscular, the hands the same, as if its hold were of uncommon strength. Its legs and feet, most delicately formed, were bare. It wore a tunic of the purest white, and round its waist was bound a lustrous belt. It held a

branch of fresh green holly in its hand, and had its dress trimmed with summer flowers. From the crown of its head there sprung a bright clear jet of light.

Scrooge: Are you the Spirit, sir, whose coming was foretold to me?

Ghost: I am!

Scrooge: Who and what are you?

Ghost: I am the Ghost of Christmas Past.

Scrooge: Long past?

Ghost: No. Your past.

Scrooge: What brings you here?

Ghost: Your welfare! Rise, and walk with me!

Dickens: The grasp was not to be resisted. Scrooge rose, but finding that the Spirit made toward the window, he clasped its robe.

Scrooge: I am mortal, and liable to fall.

Ghost: Bear but a touch of my hand *there,* on your heart, and you shall be upheld in more than this!

Dickens: The pair passed through the wall, and stood upon an open country road, with fields on either side. The city had entirely vanished. The darkness and the mist had vanished with it, for it was a clear, cold, winter day, with snow upon the ground.

Scrooge: Good Heaven! I was bred in this place. I was a boy here!

Dickens: Scrooge was conscious of a thousand odors

floating in the air, each one connected with a thousand thoughts, and hopes, and joys, and cares long, long forgotten.

Ghost: Your lip is trembling. And what is that upon your cheek?

Scrooge: It's . . . it's a pimple . . .

Laughter rose up from the audience. Eva thought of how angry Harry had been when a zit appeared on his face.

"It's just a zit," she had said to him.

"I hate it, I hate it," he had shouted at the mirror.

"Maybe shouting at it will scare it away," Eva had said, which, even in the midst of his rage, had made him laugh.

"You think Shona won't like you," Eva had said teasingly.

"That has nothing to do with it," he said.

"Everything to do with it," Eva had replied.

And now, in the show, Harry was making everyone laugh with his "pimple."

No, not Harry, she reminded herself. *Scrooge.*
Mr. Scrooge.

Scrooge: You may lead me wherever you wish.

Ghost: You recollect the way?

Scrooge: Remember it! I could walk it blindfolded.

Ghost: Strange to have forgotten it for so many
            years! Let us go on.

After a long silence in the dark, François asked,
"Why was he called Stinker?"

"Not for the reason you might think." Ray
laughed. "I used to go over to their place evenings,
weekends, and have a great time. Once their tub was
blocked and I was there when a plumber was over,

under the tub. My friend asked the plumber how he was doing, and the plumber said, 'Well, sonny, it's a real stinker.' Anyway, my friend came back into the room, and his mom asked him how the plumber was doing, and my friend said, in front of all of us, 'Well, sonny, it's a real stinker.' He sounded so much like the plumber we fell over laughing and laughing. We were only around seven. Imagine that, all you have to do when you're that young is say something like that, and the whole world seems hilarious. 'Ha! Well, sonny, it's a real stinker.' I've never forgotten that."

Scrooge: Walking along this road, I recognize every gate, and post, and tree. That little market town in the distance, with its bridge, its church and winding river. And these boys coming by in great spirits, these merry travelers — I knew them, every one.

Ghost: These are but shadows of the things that have been. They do not know we are here.

Dickens: Why was Scrooge overjoyed beyond all bounds to see them? Why did his cold eye glisten, and his heart leap up as they went past? Why was he filled with gladness when he heard them give each other Merry Christmas, as they parted at crossroads and byways, for their several homes? What was Merry Christmas to Scrooge? Out upon Merry Christmas! What good had it ever done to him? The pair soon approached a mansion of dull red brick, with a little dome, with a weather vane on the top, and a bell hanging in it. It was a large house, but one of broken fortunes: for the spacious offices were little used, their walls were damp and mossy, their windows broken, and their gates decayed. Entering the dreary hall, they found the house to be cold and vast. They went across the hall, to a door at the back of the house. It opened to a long, bare, melancholy room, made barer still by lines of plain wooden benches and desks.

At one of these a lonely boy, neglected by his friends, was reading near a feeble fire.

Scrooge: Poor boy! That's me, sitting there. I wish . . . but it's too late now.

Ghost: What is the matter?

Scrooge: Nothing. Nothing.

Dickens: The Ghost smiled thoughtfully and waved its hand.

A drip landed on the table in front of them. The rain was so heavy that it even found a way to get in around the edge of the skylight above them.

Ray groped his way over to the garbage can in the corner, took out an empty paper coffee cup, and brought it back to the table. He placed it where the drop of rainwater had fallen on the table.

"Ha! When Lisa and I got together, you know,

we were in an apartment on the top floor of an old tenement building. We took the leaks for everyone below us. We would lie in bed listening to the music of the drips falling into the pots and pans we had laid on the floor to catch them . . . *Ping, pong, pong, ping.* She said it was jazz . . . our jazz."

They listened to the sound of the drips falling into the cup.

More like "bock" than "pong" or "ping," Ray thought. "Do you know what my kids like hearing about most, François?"

"How you and Lisa got together, I suppose."

"Not really. They're more interested in the time just after that. What it was like when it was just us two without them. It's like they think it's some kind of time we're not entitled to have. I tell them about that jazz with the drips. I tell them, and it's true, I couldn't believe my luck. All through my teens, I was the geek kid. Girls used to use me to hide behind, so that they could peek around me to get a view of some other guy. At college, everyone would go off in pairs apart from me. But then, hey! I got with someone who wanted ME! I tell the kids that. And they laugh. Eva says, 'Mom must have been crazy. Why would you want HIM?'"

Bock!

Another drip landed in the coffee cup.

Ghost: Let us see another Christmas!

Dickens: Scrooge's former self grew larger at the words, and there he was, alone again, when all the other boys had gone home for the jolly holidays.

(*A little girl, much younger than the boy, comes darting in, puts her arms about his neck, kisses him . . .*)

Girl: Dear, dear brother! I have come to bring you home, dear brother! To bring you home, home, home!

Boy: Home, little Fan?

Girl: Yes! Home, for good and all. Home, forever and ever. Father is so much kinder than he used to be, that home's like Heaven! He spoke so gently to me one dear night when I was going to bed, that I was not afraid to ask him once more if you might come home, and he said, "Yes, you should," and sent me in a coach to bring you. And you're to be a man and are never to come back here; but first, we're to be together all the Christmas long, and have the merriest time in all the world.

Boy: You are quite a woman, little Fan!

Dickens: She clapped her hands and laughed, and

began to drag him, in her childish eagerness, toward the door.

Ghost: Always a delicate creature, whom a breath might have withered. But she had a large heart!

Scrooge: So she had.

Ghost: She died a woman, and had, I think, children.

Scrooge: One child.

Ghost: True. Your nephew!

Scrooge: Yes.

Dickens: They were now in a busy thoroughfare, where shadowy passengers passed and repassed, where shadowy carts and coaches battled for the way, and all the strife and

tumult of a real city were. It was made
plain enough, by the dressing of the shops,
that here, too, it was Christmastime again;
but it was evening, and the streets were
lighted up.

Ghost: Do you know this place?

Scrooge: Know it? It's old Fezziwig's! I was
           apprenticed here!

Ray looked at the paper cup. If the rain went on
long enough, it would fill up. That's what saving is
like. You collect what you get: *bock, bock, bock!*

He nodded to himself in a satisfied way, and yet
he remembered Lisa asking him, *Is there going to be
a moment, Ray, when you have enough?*

Enough. She had made the word sound a tiny bit
longer than usual.

Ray turned to François. "Tell me straight," he said,
gripping François's arm. "Do you think I'm greedy?"

"I don't know."

Ray dropped his head down onto his fist as it sat on the table. "I've never told anyone this before. I was about ten and my mom's brother was over, Uncle Phil, and they sent me out of the room. I did as I was told. They thought I had gone to my room. I did, but then I crept back and listened through the door. They were begging Uncle Phil for money. And he was saying they hadn't paid him back for some other time. They were pleading with him. Like I say, begging. I had never heard them talk like that. They were like . . . like . . . little kids begging for presents. Then I heard Uncle Phil get up, and I scampered back to my room. When I heard the front door slam, I came out and they were crying. Both of them. I remember looking up at them and Mom saying, 'It's your uncle Phil, he's not well.' They were lying. They were lying to cover up for being so poor they had to beg for money.

"I've never told anyone that, François. I can't bear it. Everything that happened to me after that comes from that moment. I see their faces, looking down at me, saying, 'Uncle Phil, he's not well,' and in my head I hear them pleading with Phil for cash. Money. This stuff!"

Ray put his hand in his pocket, pulled out some folded bills, and threw them into the air. They disappeared into the dark on the floor.

"Imagine, if you could turn back time and I could be Uncle Phil and when they stand there saying, 'Pleeeeeease, pleeeeease,' I just hand them a wad of cash."

They went on sitting in the dark, listening to Ray breathing deeply.

"Why don't you go back to the show?" François said. "Go back."

Scrooge: Why, it's old Fezziwig! Bless his heart, it's Fezziwig alive again!

(Old Fezziwig lays down his pen and looks up at the clock, which is pointing to the hour of seven.)

Fezziwig: Yo ho, there! Ebenezer! Dick!

Scrooge: There am I! And Dick Wilkins, to be sure! Bless me, yes. There he is. He was very much attached to me, was Dick. Dear, dear!

Fezziwig: Yo ho, my boys! No more work tonight. Christmas Eve, Dick. Christmas, Ebenezer! Let's have the shutters up, before a man can say, Jack Robinson! Clear away, my lads, and let's have lots of room here! Hilli-ho, Dick! Chirrup, Ebenezer!

Dickens: Clear away! There was nothing they wouldn't have cleared away, or couldn't have cleared away, with old Fezziwig looking on.

It was done in a minute. Every movable was packed off, the floor was swept, the lamps were trimmed, fuel was heaped upon the fire, and the warehouse was as snug, and warm, and dry, and bright a ballroom as you would desire to see upon a winter's night. In came a fiddler and went up to the lofty desk, and made an orchestra of it. In came Mrs. Fezziwig, one vast substantial smile. In came the three Miss Fezziwigs, beaming and lovable. In came the six young followers whose hearts they broke. In came all the young men and women employed in the business. In came the housemaid, with her cousin, the baker. In came the cook, with her brother's particular friend, the milkman. In came the boy from over the way, trying to hide himself behind the girl from next door. In they all came, one after another. There were dances, and there were forfeits, and more dances, and there was cake, and there was a great piece of cold roast, and there was a great piece of cold boiled, and there were mince pies, and plenty of beer. When the clock struck eleven, this domestic ball broke up. Mr. and Mrs. Fezziwig took their stations, one on either side of the door, and shaking hands with every person individually as he or she went out, wished him or her a Merry Christmas. Thus the cheerful voices died away, and the lads were left to their beds, which were under a counter in the back shop.

Ghost: A small matter, to make these silly folks so full of gratitude.

Scrooge: Small?

Ghost: Old Mr. Fezziwig has spent but a few pounds: three or four perhaps. Is that so much that he deserves all the praise being afforded him?

Scrooge: It isn't that. It isn't that, Spirit. Mr. Fezziwig has the power to render us happy or unhappy, to make our work light or heavy, a pleasure or a toil. Say that his power lies in words and looks, in things so slight and insignificant that it is impossible to add and count 'em up: what then? The happiness he gives is quite as great as if it cost a fortune. I . . . er.

Ghost: What is the matter?

Scrooge: Nothing particular.

Ghost: Something, I think?

Scrooge: No. No. I should like to be able to say a word or two to my clerk just now! That's all.

"There's something that Lisa and I never tell the

kids, you know," said Ray, "though sometimes I wonder if they've got some inkling of it . . ."

"Ray," said François, "just go back. Tell me another time. I can do this here."

Ray couldn't be stopped. Sometimes the compulsion to tell is greater than the compulsion to do.

"When little Eva says, 'What was it like with you two—'"

"Little Eva!" François interrupted. "I just got it. She's named for the singer, yes?"

"Yes, yes, she's our little Eva. Lisa and I used to dance to 'The Loco-Motion' . . . Look, not that, not that. What I'm talking about is the time Lisa left me. We don't tell the kids that. After she was gone and I used to sit in the apartment with the leaks — what did you call them, the water escaping? — yes, like her. She escaped. And I used to imagine her in a beautiful house, with a beautiful husband, surrounded by beautiful children, and it drove me crazy. It drove me completely crazy."

"Talking Heads."

"What?"

"The band. David Byrne."

"I know. I know. I know," Ray said. "'Once in a Lifetime.' I know it. It's about me. All that 'beautiful house' stuff. Just like me. Thinking I had it all."

François started singing and humming the song under his breath. A minute later he said, "But she didn't go off and find all that beautiful stuff. You told me."

"No, but it was as if she did. Get it? I told myself she did, and that felt as real to me as if she really had!"

"But she does now! She's got you. You're not

getting it. Go back, for goodness' sake, Ray. Go back to the show."

But Ray didn't move. "The power'll come back on in a minute."

François sang on and on.

Ghost: My time grows short. Quick!

Dickens: Again Scrooge saw himself. He was older now — a man in the prime of life. His face had not the harsh and rigid lines of later years, but it had begun to wear the signs of greed. There was an eager, restless movement in the eye, which showed the passion that had taken root. He was not alone, but sat by the side of a fair young girl in whose eyes there were tears, which sparkled in the light.

Girl: It matters little. To you, very little. I matter little, for another idol has displaced me.

81

Younger Scrooge: What idol has displaced you?

Girl: A golden one.

Younger Scrooge: This is the way of the world! There
is nothing so hard as poverty, and yet there
is nothing the world condemns so much as
the pursuit of wealth!

Girl: I have seen your kinder aspirations fall off
one by one, until the master passion, Gain,
has taken over. Have I not seen that?

Younger Scrooge: What then? Even if I have grown so
much wiser, what then? I am not changed
toward you, Belle. Am I?

Girl: You *are* changed. When we fell in with each
other, you were another man.

Younger Scrooge: I was a boy.

Girl: Your own feeling tells you that you were not
            what you are. I am. How often I have thought
            of this, I will not say. It is enough that I *have*
            thought of it. I would gladly think otherwise
            if I could. Heaven knows! May you be happy
            in the life you have chosen!

Dickens: She left him.

Scrooge: Spirit! Show me no more! Conduct me
            home. Why do you delight to torture me?

Ghost: One shadow more!

Eva shuddered. Lisa thought Eva was cold, so she
silently held up a shawl she had brought and raised
questioning eyebrows at Eva.

   Eva smiled, shook her head, and pointed at the
stage as if to say, *The shivering, shuddering stuff
is coming from there, what with it all being so . . .
so . . . grim!*

"Do you know why Lisa left me?" Ray said in a quiet monotone.

"You're not listening to me, Ray. Go back to the play!" François's voice was urgent.

"She said I had a 'one-track mind,' but—but— then she said, 'Where am I in this great scheme of things, Ray?'"

François didn't want to go through it again and shouted at Ray: "But she came back! Not many guys in your situation are as lucky. Don't you get it? But you might not get another chance. Do you remember how you painted a picture of her somewhere else, in another setup, having a beautiful life? It could happen."

Scrooge: No more! No more. I don't wish to see it. Show me no more!

Dickens: But the relentless Ghost pinioned Scrooge

in both his arms and forced him to observe what happened next. They were in another scene and place: a room, not very large or handsome, but full of comfort. Near to the winter fire sat a beautiful young girl, so like that last that Scrooge believed it was the same, until he saw *her*, now a comely matron, sitting opposite her daughter. The noise in this room was tumultuous, for there were more children there than Scrooge could count; they were not forty children conducting themselves like one, but every child was conducting itself like forty. But no one seemed to care; on the contrary, the mother and daughter laughed heartily, and enjoyed it very much.

Harry watched Shona as she said this and remembered Miss Cavani encouraging Shona with, "This is you, folks! This is what you're all like. Show us, Shona dear, what 'tumultuous' feels like."

In the audience, Lisa winked at Eva.

Yeah, all right Mom, Eva thought. *Every time some author says "mother and daughter" doesn't mean you have to say it's us. Duh!*

Scrooge: What would I not have given to be one of these children!

Dickens: But now a knocking at the door was heard, and in came the father, laden with Christmas toys and presents. Then the shouting and the struggling, and the onslaught that was made on the defenseless porter! The shouts of wonder and delight with which every package was received! By degrees, the children and their emotions got out of the parlor, by one stair at a time, up to the top of the house, where they went to bed.

The master of the house sat down with his daughter and her mother at the fireside.

Scrooge (*looking at the daughter*): That a creature like that, just as graceful and as full of promise, might have called me father . . .

Husband: Belle, I saw an old friend of yours this afternoon.

Belle: Who was it?

Husband: Guess!

Belle: How can I? Tut, don't I know . . . Mr. Scrooge?

Husband: Mr. Scrooge it was. I passed his office window and as it was not shut up, and he had a candle inside, I could scarcely help seeing him. His partner lies upon the point of death, I hear, and there he sat alone. Quite alone in the world, I do believe.

Scrooge: Spirit! Remove me from this place.

Ghost: I told you these were shadows of the things that have been. That they are what they are, do not blame me!

Scrooge: Remove me! I cannot bear it! Leave me! Take me back. Haunt me no longer!

This was one of Harry's favorite lines. He loved shouting, "Haunt me no longer!" and waiting for a second before the lights went out and the auditorium went dark.

He paused for a moment, looking out into the dark of the auditorium, full of a weary sadness that Dad wasn't there to hear that line float out into the crowd; he wasn't there to hear the great wave of applause that came a beat later.

Harry crept off the stage while the clapping continued. As he crept and crouched, it almost felt like he was an old man, and he wondered if, when Dad was old and he, Harry, was a man, Dad would tell him how sad he was he missed Harry being Scrooge?

Then as Harry made his way into the Green Room, and he burst into the backstage buzz and bustle, the thought vanished.

Sunil thumped him on the back. "It's going great, Grubby."

Harry really didn't mind Sunil calling him that. Even more pleasing was the glance that Shona sneaked toward him around the edge of Désol'é's arm.

"Miss!" Rasheda burst out to Miss Cavani. "My mom's brought all her cousin's family. There's about ten of them!"

"That's what it's all for, darling," Miss Cavani said, smiling.

Keep focused, Harry said to himself, lifting the mask off his face, giving himself a wipe, and putting it back on . . .

Chapter 3

*J*ime! Time!" Miss Cavani whispered loudly. "Throw those nerves away," she added in her sprightly way, hurling imaginary nerves away from herself in all directions.

Everyone imitated her, before subsiding into silent, concentrated expectation for the start of Stave Three.

Do it, Harry, Harry said to himself.

Dickens: The bell struck one, and when no shape appeared, Scrooge was taken with a violent fit of trembling. Five minutes, ten minutes, a quarter of an hour went by, yet nothing came.

Scrooge (*walking toward the doorway*): But what is the source of that blaze of ruddy light, I wonder?

Ghost: Ebenezer Scrooge! Come in, come in.

Dickens: It was Scrooge's own room. There was no doubt about that. But it had undergone a surprising transformation. The walls and ceiling were so hung with living green that it looked a perfect grove, from every part of which bright gleaming berries glistened. The crisp leaves of holly, mistletoe, and ivy reflected back the light, and a blaze went roaring up the chimney. Heaped up on the floor, to form a kind of throne, were

turkeys, geese, poultry, great joints of meat, sucking-pigs, long wreaths of sausages, mince pies, plum puddings, barrels of oysters, red-hot chestnuts, cherry-cheeked apples, juicy oranges, luscious pears, and seething bowls of punch. Upon this couch, there sat a jolly giant, glorious to see.

Ghost: Come in! Come in and know me better, man! I am the Ghost of Christmas Present. Look upon me! You have never seen the like of me before!

Scrooge: Never.

Ghost: Have you never walked forth with my elder brothers born in these later years?

Scrooge: I don't think I have. I am afraid I have not. Have you had many brothers, Spirit?

Ghost: More than eighteen hundred.

Scrooge: A tremendous family to provide for!

Ghost: Come!

Scrooge: Spirit, conduct me where you will. I went forth last night, and I learned a lesson which is working now. Tonight, if you have anything to teach me, let me profit by it.

Ghost: Touch my robe!

Dickens: Scrooge did as he was told, and held it fast. All vanished instantly.

The lights had come back on in the industrial park; the computers were humming.

François realized that Ray was intent on ignoring his plea to go back. He had been touched by the emotion in Ray's voice as he had talked about what it had been like to meet Lisa and to have feared losing her in that time before Harry was born. Out of the corner of his eye, François could see that Ray's eyes were fixed on one of the screens as if there was some deep power behind the flickering light, pulling him in.

"The file with the other data on it . . ." Ray muttered half to himself, half to François.

François was leaning back, looking at the ceiling. He was wondering what it would take to change Ray's mind.

"It's not here."

François responded without taking his eyes off the ceiling. "You didn't upload it. It's on your laptop."

The moment Ray heard "laptop," he leapt up like a startled dog and smacked the side of his own head. "I'll go home and get it!"

François smiled to himself. Why could his friend not see the irony of it? A whole world of feelings about life couldn't budge him one little inch; the single word *laptop* made him jump like a firecracker. Then again, perhaps the mysterious Ray could see the irony and chose to ignore it.

With a quick shake of his car key and a quick

squeeze of François's shoulder, Ray was out the door. He strode across the parking lot, watched by the gray UFOs of the office units.

Mrs. Cratchit: What has ever kept your precious father, then? And your brother, Tiny Tim! And Martha warn't as late last Christmas Day by half an hour!

Martha: Here's Martha, Mother!

Young Cratchits: Here's Martha, Mother! Hurrah! There's *such* a goose, Martha!

Mrs. Cratchit: Why, bless your heart alive, my dear, how late you are!

Martha: We'd a deal of work to finish up last night, and had to clear away this morning, Mother!

Mrs. Cratchit: Well! Never mind so long as you are

come. Sit ye down before the fire, my dear, and have a warm, Lord bless ye!

Young Cratchits: No, no! There's Father coming. Hide, Martha, hide!

Dickens: So Martha hid herself, and in came Bob the father, and Tiny Tim upon his shoulder.

Bob: Why, where's our Martha?

Mrs. Cratchit: Not coming.

Bob: Not coming? Not coming upon Christmas Day? Ah! There she is!

(Martha comes out from behind the closet door and runs into Bob's arms, while the two young Cratchits hustle Tiny Tim and bear him off into the wash house.)

Mrs. Cratchit: And how did little Tim behave?

Bob: As good as gold, and better. Somehow he gets thoughtful, sitting by himself so much, and thinks the strangest things you ever heard. He told me, coming home, that he hoped the people saw him in the church, because he was a cripple, and it might be pleasant to them to remember upon Christmas Day, He who made lame beggars walk, and blind men see.

The woman next to Lisa leaned across to Eva and nodded at her.

Oh, for goodness' sake, Eva thought. *Just because someone says the word* lame, *it doesn't mean you have to nod away at me.*

Lisa felt Eva tense up beside her like a cat watching an intruder cat through a window.

Lisa smiled back at the woman . . . and immediately regretted doing it, as she knew that Eva would tell her later why it was annoying.

Dickens: Such a bustle followed that you might have thought a goose the rarest of all birds; a feathered phenomenon; and in truth it was something very like it in that house. (*The children return to help set dinner.*) At last the dishes were set on, and grace was said. It was followed by a breathless pause, as Mrs. Cratchit, looking slowly all along the carving knife, prepared to plunge it in the breast; but when she did, and when the long expected gush of stuffing issued forth, one murmur of delight arose all round the board, and even Tiny Tim, excited by the two young Cratchits, beat on the table with the handle of his knife, and feebly cried:

Tiny Tim: Hurrah!

Bob: I don't believe there ever was such a goose cooked.

Once again, Ray was speeding down the road in the car. This time his mind was focused on the laptop. Where had he put it? In spite of his fear that vital data could be lost or corrupted, he did let Eva — no one else, only Eva — use it on occasion. The feeling of sheer eye-watering joy he got from seeing Eva poring over it overcame any feelings of caution. The day she found the YouTube video of a cat seeming to sing to the TV was one of the happiest moments  of his life. How could such a thing make her scream with laughter so much, for so long? In that moment, it was as if she banished all pain, all sadness, all dreariness. *If only you could package that magic,* he thought, *open it up, eat it, and, hey— happy. Wow, if you could do that, you really would mint it.*

As he thought *eat,* Ray felt a pang. Come to think of it, he was hungry. Tomorrow, Christmas dinner. A few years ago, he would have known every single detail of what to expect because he had been the family's Christmas shopper, but now Lisa did it with Harry.

Ray remembered how one time he stood in the supermarket in front of a wall of Christmas goodies and was hit at that very moment by what felt like an electric shock: how different this was from his own childhood, where every treat, every present, every little luxury came with a warning—his mother reminding them of how lucky they were that they weren't standing in a line at a soup kitchen, how fortunate they were they weren't begging in the street. Ha!—that time Stinker was over and Ray's mother went to the cabinet and took out a bar of chocolate. Not two bars: one bar. She broke it in half and handed a half to each of them.

But Ray knew there was another bar in there. He had seen his mother put the two bars in the cabinet. So he said, "Mom, can we have the other bar too?"

She was furious. "Do you have any idea, any idea at all, how lucky you are? Instead of being content that you've got any chocolate at all, you're feeling sorry for yourself that you haven't got a bar each? Just eat what I've given you and Stinker and be thankful. That's not so hard, is it?"

Well, actually, it was hard. It was hard to be thankful when someone was telling you to be thankful. All through his childhood, Ray felt as if he had never been allowed to enjoy anything in some clear, pure way. The joy of having a new pair of shoes or having a nice piece of chicken came filtered through feelings of relief that they weren't ill or starving or dying. Though he never confessed it to anyone around him, Ray knew exactly how it made him feel: angry. Angry that his mother hadn't let him enjoy things, and he turned that anger against the very people who were less fortunate than they were. It wasn't his mother who was spoiling his fun; it was all these poor and sick people she seemed to parade in front of him every time he had a cookie.

Once he had seen a homeless guy at the entrance to the train station and imagined a garbage truck stopping next to him, a couple of the guys getting out in their orange vests, grabbing the guy and slinging him into the back of the truck, where he was slowly taken in through the jaws. He had imagined how, if there were enough trucks like that, all swooping and grabbing and removing these people, his mother couldn't keep telling him how lucky he wasn't like that, because there wouldn't be any of them.

Wow, then every cookie would taste like heaven!

Bob: Oh, a wonderful pudding that was!

Mrs. Cratchit: Well, that's a weight off my mind. I confess I had had my doubts about the quantity of flour.

Dickens: Everybody had something to say about it, but nobody said or thought it was at all a small pudding for a large family. It would have been flat heresy to do so. Any Cratchit would have blushed to hint at such a thing. At last the dinner was all done, the cloth was cleared, the hearth swept, and the fire made up. Then all the Cratchit family drew round the hearth, while the chestnuts on the fire sputtered and cracked noisily.

Bob: A Merry Christmas to us all, my dears. God bless us!

Everyone: God bless us all!

Tiny Tim: God bless us, every one!

At that, a little boy down in the front called out, "God bless us, every one!" right after Tiny Tim said it, and everyone laughed. The boy was the brother of the boy playing Tiny Tim, and like Eva had spent a long time helping his brother with the lines. Miss Cavani had said to them all in the early days of rehearsals, "Doing a play like this reaches out into the lives of the whole community," and when she said that, she reached out with her hands and arms as if she herself could reach into the houses and homes of them all.

Scrooge: Spirit, tell me if Tiny Tim will live.

Ghost: I see an empty seat, in the poor chimney corner, and a crutch without an owner, carefully preserved. If these shadows remain unaltered by the future, the child will die.

Scrooge: No, no, oh, no, kind Spirit! Say he will be spared.

Ghost: If these shadows remain unaltered by the

future, what then? If he be like to die, he had better do it, and decrease the surplus population.

Dickens: Scrooge hung his head to hear his own words quoted by the Spirit, and was overcome with penitence and grief.

As the car rolled along the highway, Ray thought back to the boy he was, with his dream of the trucks. He recalled lying in bed making the world simple. Everyone would live in a house with a front and back yard. He hated watching TV when they did all those charity things where TV stars tried to sing famous songs, and they would cut to the star standing next to a kid dying somewhere. *That dying child wasn't my fault*, he'd think, and with a magic sweep, one of his trucks would clear it all away. And, yes, everyone would live in a house with a back and front yard.

Was I really that boy? Did I have that streak

inside me? He felt a flush of embarrassment creep up the right-hand side of his neck. *I was! I was that boy. I did think that stuff. Why is this night getting so complicated?*

Bob: Mr. Scrooge! I'll give you Mr. Scrooge, the Founder of the Feast!

Mrs. Cratchit: The Founder of the Feast indeed! I wish he were here. I'd give him a piece of my mind to feast upon, and I hope he'd have a good appetite for it.

Bob: My dear, the children — Christmas Day.

Mrs. Cratchit: It should be Christmas Day, I am sure, on which one drinks the health of such an odious, stingy, hard, unfeeling man as Mr. Scrooge. You know he is, Robert! Nobody knows it better than you do, poor fellow!

Bob: My dear — Christmas Day.

Mrs. Cratchit: I'll drink his health for your sake and the Day's, not for his. Long life to him. A Merry Christmas and a Happy New Year! He'll be very merry and very happy, I have no doubt!

Dickens: Scrooge was the ogre of the family. The mention of his name cast a dark shadow on the party, which was not dispelled for a full five minutes. After it had passed away, they were ten times merrier than before, from the mere relief of Scrooge the Baleful being done with.

Bob: I have my eye on a job for you, Peter, which would bring in full five-and-sixpence weekly.

Young Cratchit: Peter? A man of business?

Peter: I don't see what's so funny about that . . .

Martha: Oh, but children, work is nothing like your pretend fun and games . . .

Dickens: Martha, who was a poor apprentice at a milliner's, then told them what kind of work she had to do, and how many hours she worked at a stretch, and how she meant to lie a-bed tomorrow morning for a good long rest, tomorrow being a holiday she passed at home. And bye and bye they had a song from Tiny Tim, who had a plaintive little voice, and sang it very well indeed. There was nothing of high mark in all of this. They were not a handsome family; they were not well dressed. But they were happy, grateful, pleased with one another, and contented with the time, and when they faded, and looked happier yet in the bright sprinklings of the Spirit's torch at parting, Scrooge had his eye upon them, and especially on Tiny Tim, until the last.

Eva knew enough about herself to know that she loved dramas: real-life or in stories, small or large, silly or serious. Before Harry came home with the play and they started rehearsing at home, she didn't know the story of *A Christmas Carol*. Even though she had loved playing the parts to help Harry, seeing it up onstage in the lights, with the makeup and the masks, with the arrival of the ghosts, first of Marley, then of Christmas Past, and now of the Present . . . it was all like a powerful magic. In a way, this was like the YouTube of the past. The Ghosts could in their own way bring up scenes and show them to Scrooge. She remembered how she loved finding the singing cat.

Nephew: Ha, ha! Ha, ha, ha!

Dickens: If you should happen, by any unlikely chance, to know a man more blest with a laugh than Scrooge's nephew, all I can say is, I should like to know him too. Introduce him to me, and I'll cultivate his acquaintance.

Nephew's Wife: Ha, ha! Ha, ha, ha, ha!

Nephew: He said that Christmas was a humbug, as I live! He believed it too!

Nephew's Wife: More shame on him, Fred!

Nephew: He's a comical old fellow, that's the truth, and not so pleasant as he might be. However, his offenses carry their own punishment, and I have nothing to say against him.

Nephew's Wife: I'm sure he is very rich, Fred. At least you always tell *me* so.

Nephew: What of that, my dear! His wealth is of no use to him. He doesn't do any good with it. He doesn't make himself comfortable with it. He hasn't the satisfaction of thinking — ha, ha, ha! — that he is ever going to benefit *us* with it.

Nephew's Wife: I have no patience with him.

Nephew: Oh, I have! I am sorry for him; I couldn't be angry with him if I tried. Who suffers by his ill whims? Himself, always. Here, he takes it into his head to dislike us, and he won't come and dine with us. What's the consequence? He doesn't lose much of a dinner.

Nephew's Wife: Indeed, I think he loses a very good dinner.

Nephew: Well! I'm very glad to hear it. I was only going to say, I mean to give him the same chance every year, whether he likes it or not, for I pity him. He may complain about Christmas till he dies, but he can't help thinking better of it if he finds me going there, in good temper, year after year, and saying, "Uncle Scrooge, how are you?"

Ahead on the road, Ray's headlights picked out the sign: one way toward home, the other toward Harry's school. In his head, Ray heard François say to him, *Go back. Go to the show.*

At a slight touch of the wheel, the car would go that route. That's all it would take.

But then the thought of his laptop flicking open, the cursor finding the file, the file opening up, the data he needed to send to Mumbai traveling thousands of miles in a few seconds, was enough to make Ray turn the wheel toward home.

No, Ray said to himself, and his hands tightened on the steering wheel, *I don't have to do what François or anyone else tells me to. I'm me. This is not about making my mind up about something right in the here and now. This is about the bigger picture. I can see that bigger picture, and I'm sticking with it.*

He felt himself nod, as if there were another Ray right there with him in the car and that Ray was agreeing with Ray.

Nod. *Yes, Ray.*

Dickens: It was a game called Yes and No, where Scrooge's nephew had to think of something, and the rest must find out what; he only answering to their questions yes or no.

Partygoer: An animal?

Nephew: Yes.

Partygoer: A live animal?

Nephew: Yes.

Partygoer: Is it an agreeable animal?

Nephew: No.

Partygoer: A savage animal!

Nephew: Yes.

Partygoer: An animal that grunts and growls sometimes?

Nephew: Yes.

Partygoer: Does it talk sometimes?

Nephew: Yes.

Partygoer: Does it live in a menagerie?

Nephew: No.

Partygoer: Is it ever killed in the market?

Nephew: No.

Partygoer: Does this animal live in London, and walk about the streets?

Nephew: Yes.

Partygoer: Is it a horse?

Nephew: No.

Partygoer: Is it an ass?

Nephew: Er . . . no.

There was a pause. Miss Cavani had told them, "Never be afraid of waiting. Give them time to guess."

The nephew waited. Sure enough, first a snigger and then a laugh, and a giggle from Eva.

Miss Cavani was right.

Partygoer: I have found it out! I know what it is, Fred! I know what it is!

Nephew: What is it?

Partygoer: It's your Uncle Scro-o-o-o-oge!

Dickens: Which it certainly was.

Nephew: A Merry Christmas and a Happy New Year to the old man, whatever he is! He wouldn't take it from me, but may he have it, nevertheless. To Uncle Scrooge!

Everyone: Uncle Scrooge!

Dickens: Scrooge had become so light of heart that he would have toasted the company in return, and thanked them, if the Ghost had given him time. But he and the Spirit were again upon their travels.

Much they saw, and far they went, and many homes they visited, but always with a happy end. The Spirit stood beside sickbeds, and they were cheerful; on foreign lands, and they were close at home; by struggling men, and they were patient in their greater hope; by poverty, and it was rich. In almshouse, hospital, and jail, in misery's every refuge. It was a long night, if it was only a night. For the Ghost had grown older, clearly older.

Scrooge: Are spirits' lives so short?

Ghost: My life upon this globe, is very brief. It ends tonight.

Scrooge: Tonight?

Ghost: Tonight at midnight. Hark! The time is drawing near.

(The chimes ring twelve.)

As the bells rang out, Eva leaned toward her mother. "Some people are poor now, you know."

120

Lisa nodded.

"We're not poor."

"No," Lisa agreed.

They both watched their Scrooge hurry off the stage.

"He's so good," Eva said with a sigh. Seeing Harry act so well and so convincingly seemed to make her happy and sad at the same time. Happy that the play they had rehearsed in the kitchen, in the bedroom, in the car even, was now coming alive and the auditorium of people watching were loving it so much; sad that Dad wasn't here to see it and feel it. On the occasions he did join in with things, he seemed to enjoy himself so much: that time they played Who Am I? and he couldn't guess that the bit of paper stuck to his forehead said "A caveman." Even when Harry goofed about, thumping his chest, shouting "Hoo! Hoo!" as some nutty hint, Dad had said, "A gorilla!"

He loved playing that, didn't he? Eva thought. *Imagine, by the time Harry is a man and I'm a woman, Dad will sit at home counting on his fingers how many times he was actually with us all having that kind of crazy laughing and goofing around. It was so rare, it would really be possible to count the number of times on his fingers!*

Back in the Green Room, there was a crisis. The Ghost of Christmas Yet to Come was having a breathing problem. Serena, the girl who played him, had asthma.

"Back. Stand back!" Miss Cavani shouted. "For goodness' sake, let her breathe."

She snapped her fingers—it was one of her less than likable qualities—"Inhaler!"

Everyone started to hunt for Serena's inhaler. Actors, makeup people, the two boys in charge of props, everyone was turning things over—chains, rubber chickens, umbrellas, bonnets, jugs, and handbags were being moved, tipped up, pushed, pulled. There was a mighty rummaging in the pockets of jackets, coats, and pants. Serena was gasping, and Miss Cavani was flapping a towel to flush fresh cool air through the classroom window.

"Serena's mother. I saw her earlier. She's by the aisle near the front. She might have a spare, George. Purple coat."

George dashed off, hoping that there weren't many women by the aisle near the front wearing purple coats.

Harry came out of the bubble he was in, thinking of himself, of Dad, of Scrooge, and watched for a second as it seemed as if the whole cast turned into a hive of bees, tumbling over one another to help Serena.

As he looked across to Miss Cavani staying calm but active by the open window, he remembered how in the very first rehearsal she had told them that when you do a play, it's not like the rest of school where you might end up trying to do better than someone else. When you do a play, she said, everyone has to help everyone else. If someone gets something wrong, it makes the whole thing not-as-good-as-it-could-be. So we don't thank God that we're better than the person who's got something wrong, and we don't sneer at the person getting it wrong. We help them. That way everything gets better.

As Harry shook one of the shawls lying in a heap by one of the baskets, he felt something drop onto his foot. The inhaler! He hurried over to Serena and Miss Cavani.

The crisis was over.

Chapter 4

Ray clicked open the door of the house and headed for his study. Surely he had left the laptop there . . . unless someone had fetched it for Eva . . . The study was at the end of the passage, and as he hurried toward it, he had the sensation that he was more alone at this moment than he had ever been before. It was a sensation more eerie than if he had been told that he was about to go where people had heard the voices of the dead; more eerie than the night in the woods one time when he was young, hearing a hurried rushing in the bushes behind him. This wasn't the eeriness of something "out there" but the eeriness of being alone. Totally alone. After all, the rest of the family was indeed somewhere else. Enjoying themselves without him.

He reached the door of his study and the glass panels in the door looked back at him. He peeped in, half expecting to see himself in there.

Instead, he saw his room looking as if he had just left it. Room Without Ray. On the floor by his desk were his shoes, the creases on the leather uppers marked by feet no longer in the shoes. On his desk, a pen that he had not yet put back in the penholder that Lisa had bought him before they were married. It lay on the desk where he had dropped it, just before coming downstairs reluctantly, irately, angrily, when he finally agreed to go to the show.

Room Without Ray spread a cold feeling around

Ray's neck. What if the reason he wasn't there was that . . . he wasn't here? What did he even mean thinking that? He knew. He meant, what if something had happened to him . . . say, in the car, an accident, out on the highway, say . . . like, say, what happened to poor old Kwame? A crash . . . or if he had swerved off the road . . . This is what his study would look like: Room Without Ray.

And would anyone really care? Ray's study at the end of the hall . . . big deal. And Eva would have his laptop, why not? And Lisa could have the penholder, why not? And Harry, what would Harry have? The table and chair? Why not? Would they care? Would it matter to them that he wasn't here anymore?

Of course it would matter to them, he said to himself, still peering into the Room Without Ray. But hey, it was the fact that he was even asking the question that was the problem. What sort of dad was he, that he was even wondering for one millionth of a second whether his own family would care that he wasn't here anymore?

He pushed open the door to Room Without Ray.

Did it feel better that it was now Room With Ray?

Scrooge: I am in the presence of the Ghost of Christmas Yet to Come?

Dickens: The Spirit answered not, but pointed onward with its hand.

Scrooge: You are about to show me shadows of the things that have not happened, but will happen in the time before us? Is that so, Spirit? Ghost of the Future! I fear you more than any specter I have seen. But as I know your purpose is to do me good, and as I hope to live to be another man from what I was, I am prepared to stay with you, and do it with a thankful heart. Will you not speak to me?

Of all the lines in the play, "I hope to live to be another man from what I was" was the one that Harry had most wanted Dad to hear. As he said it, just like the many times he had said it in rehearsal, he had heard his own tone of voice creeping toward being Dad's voice. Not because he had ever heard Dad say anything like that. It came out that way because it was what he wanted to hear Dad say. Or something like it. He wanted Dad to give some inkling, some hint, that there was another way to live.

But then, even more than wanting Dad to hear him say that line, he had wanted Dad to see the next scene.

But he won't. He's not here.

With a great effort of mind, Harry took the anger he felt that Dad wasn't out there in the dark of the audience, and pushed it and squeezed it into Scrooge's fear and anxiety.

Dickens: It gave no reply. The hand was pointed straight before them.

Scrooge: Lead on! Lead on! The night is waning fast, and it is precious time to me, I know. Lead on, Spirit!

Dickens: They scarcely seemed to enter the city, for the city rather seemed to spring up about them. But there they were, in the heart of it: at the Royal Exchange, amongst the merchants.

Stout man: No, I don't know much about it, either way. I only know he's dead.

Another: When did he die?

Stout Man: Last night, I believe.

Third Man: Why, what was the matter with him? I thought he'd never die.

Stout Man: God knows.

Red-Faced Man: What has he done with his money?

Third Man: I haven't heard. Left it to his company, perhaps. He hasn't left it to me. That's all I know.

All: Ha, ha, ha!

Third Man: It's likely to be a very cheap funeral, for upon my life I don't know of anybody to go to it. Suppose we make up a party and volunteer?

Another: I don't mind going if a lunch is provided.

That got a laugh, Harry noticed. *Maybe they think the lunch'll be like those pre-prepared ones you get from supermarkets . . .*

No time for a silly thought like that, he reminded himself. *Focus, focus . . .*

Scrooge: What's going on? What's the explanation for this? Oh, these men, I know them. They're very important, very wealthy.

One: How are you?

Another: How are you?

One: Well! Old Scratch has got his own at last, hey?

Another: So I am told. Cold, isn't it?

One: Seasonable for Christmastime. You're not a skater, I suppose?

Another: No. No. Something else to think of. Good morning!

Scrooge: How odd. I still don't understand, Spirit. Where am I in all this?

Ray glanced around the study. There was the laptop. *Yes, Eva must have used it.* It was lying on a shelf in a place he'd never have put it. He felt a heaviness come over him, and he had a sad thought: *What if the family thinks of me not so much as Dad but as some sort of facility, nothing more than something useful?* Anything he carefully put to one side, they treated as if it were theirs. *That electronic pen thing that the guy from China gave me, Harry took that, didn't he? As if it were his. I told Eva she can use the computer, but it would be great if she put it back where she found it,* he thought. *It's not that hard, is it?*

He flicked the laptop open, and it came to life

with a metallic note plucked from the heart of Silicon Valley. Eva had changed the screen saver. It was the promotional shot from a horror film coming up in the new year starring Eva's favorite guy. Ray had heard her talking about it with Harry, something to do with a woman who is married to a guy for about ten years and slowly comes to realize that the guy's not human . . . which means that the kids aren't either . . . or are they? He laughed to himself. He knew that Harry and Eva would ask him to go and see it, and he would say he really had better things to do than sit for two hours in a theater watching grown men and women being paid millions of dollars to pretend that they're not human. Oh, please.

Oh, please. The phrase rebounded. He heard Eva saying, "Oh, please."

He looked at the face on his laptop screen. *Hell's bells, what had she done?* The horrified, ghastly face of the Hollywood actor was very slowly turning into Eva.

Scrooge: Spirit, what is this miserable den to which you have brought us? It reeks of crime and filth and misery!

(*A woman with a heavy bundle slinks into the shop. Another woman, similarly laden, comes in too, and she is closely followed by a man in faded black. All are startled by the sight of each other. After a short period of blank astonishment, they all three burst into a laugh.*)

Woman with a bundle: Let the charwoman alone to be the first! Let the laundress alone to be the second, and let the undertaker's man alone to be the third. Look here, old Joe, here's a chance! We all three meet here without meaning it!

Old Joe: You couldn't have met in a better place. Come into the parlor. Come into the parlor.

Dickens: The parlor was the space behind the screen of rags.

Woman: What odds then! What odds, Mrs. Dilber? Every person has a right to take care of themselves. He always did!

Laundress: That's true, indeed! No man more so.

Woman: Very well, then! Who's the worse for the loss of a few things like these? Not a dead man, I suppose.

Mrs. Dilber: No, indeed!

Woman: If he wanted to keep 'em after he was dead, the wicked old screw, he'd have had somebody to look after him when he was struck with Death, instead of lying gasping out his last there, alone by himself.

Mrs. Dilber: It's the truest word that ever was spoke. It's a judgment on him.

Woman: I wish it was a little heavier judgment, and

it should have been, if I could have laid my hands on anything else. Open that bundle, old Joe, and let me know the value of it. We know pretty well that we were helping ourselves, before we met here. It's no sin. Open the bundle, Joe.

Dickens: The undertaker's plunder was not extensive. A seal or two, a pencil case, a pair of sleeve buttons, and a brooch of no great value, were all.

Joe: That's your account, and I wouldn't give another sixpence, if I was to be boiled for not doing it. Who's next?'

Dickens: Mrs. Dilber was next. Sheets and towels, a little wearing apparel, two old-fashioned silver teaspoons, a pair of sugar tongs, and a few boots.

Joe: I always give too much to ladies. It's a

weakness of mine, and that's the way I ruin myself. That's your account. If you asked me for another penny, and made it an open question, I'd repent of being so liberal and knock off half a crown.

Woman: And now undo *my* bundle, Joe.

Joe: What do you call this? Bed curtains!

Mrs. Dilber: Ah! Ha, ha, ha! Bed curtains!

Joe: You don't mean to say you took them down, rings and all, with him lying there?

Woman: Yes, I do. Why not?

Joe: You were born to make your fortune, and you'll certainly do it. And these — his blankets?

Woman: Whose else's do you think? He isn't likely to take cold without 'em, I dare say.

Joe: I hope he didn't die of anything catching? Eh?

Woman: Don't you be afraid of that. I an't so fond of his company that I'd loiter about him for such things, if he did. Ah! You may look through that shirt till your eyes ache, but you won't find a hole in it, nor a threadbare place. It's the best he had, and a fine one too. They'd have wasted it, if it hadn't been for me.

Joe: What do you call wasting of it?

Woman: Putting it on him to be buried in, to be sure.
           Somebody was fool enough to do it, but I
           took it off again. If calico an't good enough
           for such a purpose, it isn't good enough for
           anything. He can't look uglier than he did
           in that one.

Scrooge: Oh! How horrible these people are!

Harry filled himself with these thoughts. What
would it really be like to see people picking up the
sheets that once wrapped your own dead body and
taking them off to sell? He shuddered to think of it,
and so the audience saw Scrooge shudder.

   The first night that he had come home with the
play, he had told Eva the whole story of the play
in one sitting, and she had listened to him without

making a sound, watching his face closely. As he told it to her, he thought that it wasn't only a ghost story — it was a horror story.

Woman: This is the end of it, you see! He frightened everyone away from him when he was alive, to profit us when he was dead! Ha, ha, ha!

Scrooge: Spirit! I see, I see. The case of this unhappy man might be my own. My life tends that way, now. Merciful Heaven, this is a fearful place. In leaving it, I shall not leave its lesson, trust me. Let us go!

The audience fell quiet, and Lisa looked slightly anxiously across to Eva. Was she all right with this? Eva, more than anyone else in the family, was in touch with the cycle of life. She went to a school where, for better or worse, the children knew that among them there were children who weren't bravely and brilliantly getting along fine; some of them were very slowly slipping away to a point at which they wouldn't come back.

Eva, the family knew, was the expert on this. It's what made her wise, Lisa decided.

Dickens: The Ghost conducted Scrooge through several streets familiar to his feet, and as they went along, Scrooge looked here and there to find his future self, but nowhere was he to be seen. They entered poor Bob Cratchit's house — the dwelling they had visited before — and found the mother and the children seated round the fire.

Peter (*reading from a book*): "And he took a child, and set him in the midst of them."

Mrs. Cratchit: Your father will be home soon.

Peter: He's late. But I think he has walked a

little slower than he used to, these few last evenings, Mother.

Mrs. Cratchit: I have known him walk with — I have known him walk with Tiny Tim upon his shoulder very fast indeed. But he was very light to carry, and his father loved him so, that it was no trouble: no trouble. (*The door rattles.*) And there is your father at the door!

Ray was about to close the laptop again and head back to the office when a little niggle in his mind told him to look at the browser's history. If Eva had been using it, what had she been looking at? He paused for a moment. *Am I being sneaky here? No, I'm being a parent. I should know what my kids look at on this machine. I wouldn't let them wander the streets, not knowing where they are, would I?*

He pulled down the menu. Sure, plenty of YouTube Singing Cat. Of course. What was this? Some medical sites. He clicked on the first one on the list. Up came a few ads, a remarkably white-toothed "doctor" talking about exactly the same condition that Eva had. *Well, that was good.* Eva wasn't taking what he or Lisa or even the consultant at the hospital was saying as gospel. She wanted to know for herself. *Hmmm.* He wondered if this really was Eva, or was it Harry, or were they looking this stuff up together?

If he'd been at home more, he'd know the answer to that one, he thought regretfully.

He read on down the text of Dr. White-Tooth. It talked about what the doctor called a "linked condition." Ray knew enough to know that this meant, "Don't go here if you want to spare yourself imagining that life is over right now."

He paused and wondered if Eva—if it was Eva—had clicked that link too. Back to the history tab—no. *Oh, that was good.*

Even so, he was drawn to the linked condition. He clicked on it and read. On and on and on, feeling himself dragged slowly into a sad scenario that he couldn't bear. *No,* he said to himself. *This can't*

happen. It isn't going to happen. It won't happen.
He looked at photos, diagrams, back to photos, and just as Eva had played around mixing the images on the screen saver, he saw Eva in every picture and diagram. Slipping away from them.

He looked up from the screen and, for half a moment, wondered where Eva was. Why couldn't he hear her in the house? Why couldn't he hear them laughing at some singing cat? *Oh, yes, they're at the show!*

And why wasn't *he* at the show? The course of the evening's events flashed in front of him in a split second, and he was overcome with a sense of things slipping between his fingers. He snapped the laptop shut, jumped up, and ran out to the car.

The laptop sat, flat and quiet, on Ray's desk.

Mrs. Cratchit: Did you go there, Robert?

Bob: Yes, my dear. I wish you could have gone too. It would have done you good to see how green a place it is. But you'll see it often. I promised him that. My little, little child! My little child! (*Sobs.*) Mr. Scrooge's nephew — now there's an extraordinarily kind man. I looked a little — just a little down, you know. He asked of me what had happened to distress me. I told him . . . He said, "I am heartily sorry for it, Mr. Cratchit, and heartily sorry for your good wife. If I can be of service to you in any way," he said, giving me his card, "that's where I live. Pray come to me." It really seemed as if he had known our Tiny Tim, and felt with us.

Mrs. Cratchit: I'm sure he's a good soul!

Bob: I shouldn't be at all surprised, mark what I say, if he got Peter a better job.

Mrs. Cratchit: Only hear that, Peter.

Girl: And then, Peter will soon be setting up for himself.

Peter: Get along with you!

Bob: It's just as likely as not, one of these days;
           though there's plenty of time for that, my
           dear. But however and whenever we part
           from each other, I am sure we shall none of
           us forget poor Tiny Tim — shall we — or
           this first parting that there was among us?

All: Never, Father!

There were times when Harry felt uncomfortable
hearing this. He hated that the story seemed to
dangle in front of his eyes the thought that he might
hear people saying, "And none of us will forget Eva,
will we?" And he felt sorry that he had even thought
those words.

Why had Miss Cavani said, "Remember, everyone, this is a story about life!"?

Bob: And I know, my dears, that when we

recollect how patient and how mild he was — although he was a little, little child — we shall not quarrel among ourselves, and forget poor Tiny Tim in doing it.

All: No, never, Father!

Scrooge: Specter, something informs me that our parting moment is at hand. I know it, but I know not how.

Dickens: The Ghost of Christmas Yet to Come conveyed Scrooge, as before.

Scrooge: Ah, yes, there! My place of occupation.

(*The Spirit stops; the hand points elsewhere.*)

Scrooge: The house is yonder. Why do you point away?

Dickens: Scrooge accompanied the ghost until they reached an iron gate.

Scrooge: A churchyard?

(*The Spirit points down to a grave. Scrooge advances toward it, trembling.*)

Before I draw nearer to that stone to which you point, answer me one question. Are these the shadows of the things that will be, or are they shadows of things that may be, only?

Dickens: Still the Ghost pointed downward to the grave by which it stood.

(*The gravestone is lit, revealing: "Ebenezer Scrooge"*)

Scrooge: Is this . . . Am I that man they spoke of in the street, and in that wretched den?

(The Spirit's finger points from the grave to Scrooge, and back again.)

No, Spirit! Oh no, no! Spirit! Hear me! I
am not the man I was. I will not be the man
I would certainly have been but for these
events. Why show me this, if I am past all
hope? Good Spirit, your nature pities me.
Assure me that I yet may change these

shadows you have shown me, by an altered life! I will honor Christmas in my heart, and try to keep it all the year. I will live in the past, the present, and the future. The Spirits of all three shall strive within me. I will not shut out the lessons that they teach. Oh, tell me I may sponge away the writing on this stone!

Harry caught sight of Lisa's and Eva's faces in the white moonlight cast from the stage. He had never felt so proud, so strong as he did at that moment. Maybe Dad wouldn't ever understand what really matters. At the end of the day, what mattered here was that Harry himself was understanding it.

He was getting the point of what Scrooge had discovered.

Chapter 5

The End of It

R ay revved the car and pushed it faster.

At the light, he rummaged in the old CD case in the glove compartment and nearly pulled out some ancient thing the kids had loved when they were much younger, something to do with Captain Banana and the Banana Skins.

He smiled.

Hey, I smiled, he thought, and his fingers found their way to an old soul album that he and Lisa used to play. It was near the top, which must have been because Lisa had played it the last time she was using the car on her own — Sam Cooke: "A Change Is Gonna Come."

Ha!

The lights changed.

Ray pushed the car on.

Scrooge: I will live in the past, the present, and the future! The Spirits of all three shall strive within me. Oh, Jacob Marley! Heaven and the Christmas Time be praised for this! I say it on my knees, old Jacob — on my knees! These bed curtains — they are not torn down, they are not torn down, rings and all. They are here; I am here: the shadows of the things that would have been may be dispelled. They will be. I know they will! I don't know what to do! I am as light

as a feather; I am as happy as an angel; I am as merry as a schoolboy. A Merry Christmas to everybody! A Happy New Year to all the world! Hallo here! Whoop! Hallo! There's the door, by which the Ghost of Jacob Marley entered! There's the corner where the Ghost of Christmas Present sat! There's the window where I saw the wandering Spirits! It's all right, it's all true, it all happened. Ha, ha, ha!

Harry felt real joy. Of course it was sad that Dad wasn't here, but now Harry knew that he had to feel strong enough in himself and not just see himself as missing something or lacking something. Mom and Eva shone in the light of what he was doing, and Miss Cavani too.

He looked across at Shona. She, too, answered and replied to him onstage now in the performance more than she had done at any point in the rehearsal.

He felt her look and it was a moment he wanted to keep deep inside him.

What Harry didn't know, though, was that Ray had crept into the back of the auditorium.

Dickens: Really, for a man who had been out of practice for so many years, it was a splendid laugh, a most illustrious laugh. The father of a long, long line of brilliant laughs!

Scrooge: I don't know what day of the month it is! I don't know how long I've been among the Spirits. I don't know anything. I'm quite a baby. Never mind. I don't care. I'd rather be a baby. Hallo! Whoop! Hallo here!

(*Church bells ring outside.*)

Scrooge: Oh, glorious, glorious! (*Opens window.*) Golden sunlight; heavenly sky; sweet fresh air; merry bells. Oh, glorious. Glorious! What's today?

Boy: Eh?

Scrooge: What's today, my fine fellow?

Boy: Today? Why, Christmas Day.

Scrooge: It's Christmas Day! I haven't missed it. The Spirits have done it all in one night. They can do anything they like. Of course they can. Of course they can. Hallo, my fine fellow!

Boy: Hallo!

Scrooge: Do you know the poulterer's, in the next street but one, at the corner?

Boy: I do.

Scrooge: An intelligent boy! A remarkable boy! Do you know whether they've sold the prize turkey that was hanging up there? Not the little prize turkey — the big one?

Boy: What, the one as big as me?

Scrooge: What a delightful boy! It's a pleasure to talk to him. Yes, my buck!

Boy: It's hanging there now.

Scrooge: Is it? Go and buy it.

Boy: Walk-er!

Scrooge: No, no, I am in earnest. Go and buy it, and tell 'em to bring it here, that I may give them directions where to take it. Come back with the man, and I'll give you a shilling. Come back with him in less than five minutes, and I'll give you half a crown!

Scrooge (*to himself*): I'll send it to Bob Cratchit's! He shan't know who sends it. It's twice the size of Tiny Tim.

Dickens: The chuckle with which he said this, and the chuckle with which he paid for the turkey when the poulterer's man arrived, and the chuckle with which he paid for the cab, and the chuckle with which he recompensed the boy, were only to be exceeded by the chuckle with which he sat down breathless in his chair again, and chuckled till he cried.

Ray, hiding in the gloom at the back of the hall, could hardly believe his eyes or ears! Where was the little boy who had stood by the car, sniffing over his broken mask? Gone. Somewhere in among that Victorian costume, behind that Scrooge half-mask, he could see and hear a strong, confident, happy voice. And it wasn't just because he had to pretend. Ray was sure of that. This was the sound of someone glad that he had just discovered a new place.

He may not have been there to see exactly how or when or why he had done it, Ray thought, but at least he was here to see that it had just happened. He moved toward Lisa and Eva . . . then stopped himself. Why should I interrupt them? He could see from behind how absorbed they were in the show.

Dickens: Scrooge dressed himself all in his best,

and at last got out into the streets. The people were by this time pouring forth, as he had seen them with the Ghost of Christmas Present — and walking with his hands behind him, Scrooge regarded every one with a delighted smile. He looked so irresistibly pleasant, in a word, that three or four good-humored fellows said:

Fellows: Good morning, sir! A Merry Christmas to you!

Dickens: And Scrooge said often afterward, that of all the happy sounds he had ever heard, those were the happiest in his ears.

Scrooge: My dear sir, how do you do? I hope you succeeded yesterday. It was very kind of you. A Merry Christmas to you, sir!

Gentleman: Mr. Scrooge?

164

Scrooge: Yes, that is my name, and I fear it may not be pleasant to you. Allow me to ask your pardon. And will you have the goodness —

(Scrooge whispers in his ear.)

Gentleman: Lord bless me! My dear Mr. Scrooge, are you serious?

Scrooge: If you please. Not a farthing less. A great many back payments are included in it, I assure you. Will you do me that favor?

Gentleman Two: My dear sir, I don't know what to say to such munifi —

Scrooge: Don't say anything, please. Come and see me. Will you come and see me?

Gentleman: I will!

Scrooge: Thank'ee. I am much obliged to you. I thank you fifty times. Bless you!

Dickens: He went to church, and walked about the streets, and watched the people hurrying to and fro, and patted children on the head, and questioned beggars, and found that everything could yield him pleasure. He had never dreamed that any walk — that anything — could give him so much happiness. In the afternoon he turned his steps toward his nephew's house.

Scrooge: Fred!

Nephew: Why bless my soul! Who's that?

Scrooge: It's I. Your Uncle Scrooge. I have come to dinner. Will you let me in, Fred?

Dickens: Let him in! It is a mercy Fred didn't shake his arm off. Scrooge was made to feel at home in five minutes. Nothing could be heartier. Wonderful party, wonderful games, wonderful unanimity, won-der-ful happiness!

For just a moment, Harry's mind wandered away from Shona being Dickens, wandered away from the play altogether, forward to tomorrow. Surely Dad wouldn't need to go to the office tomorrow. No, he knew that the people doing business in Mumbai wouldn't necessarily be off for Christmas, but surely, surely Dad would want to be there, when they ripped open the presents and sang carols . . . when they tried to make up their own, when Nan and Granddad would sit there not getting the lyrics, which was always, always, the best part of the morning.

He imagined himself and Eva tying Dad to the table so that he couldn't suddenly look at his phone and say that he had to dash off and wouldn't be long. That he couldn't go out the door, a cloud of disappointment settling over the table.

Dickens: Scrooge was early at the office next morning. Oh, he was early there. If he could only be there first, and catch Bob Cratchit coming late! That was the thing he had set his heart upon. And he did it; yes, he did! The clock struck nine. No Bob. A quarter past. No Bob. He was a full eighteen minutes and a half behind his time. Scrooge sat with his door wide open, that he might see him come in.

Harry heard Miss Cavani's voice in his head. "This is the hardest part of the play, Harry!" What she meant is that he had to go all the way back to the mean, pinched, nasty Scrooge here. Everyone in the hall watching, everyone in the play, had to believe this was old Scrooge come back and that he hadn't changed.

Scrooge: Hallo! What do you mean by coming here at this time of day?

Bob: I am very sorry, sir, I *am* behind my time.

Scrooge: You are? Yes. I think you are. Step this way, if you please.

Bob: It's only once a year, sir. It shall not be repeated. I was making rather merry yesterday, sir.

Scrooge: Now, I'll tell you what, my friend. I am not going to stand this sort of thing any longer. And therefore, and therefore, I am about to raise your salary!

The little boy up front who had called out Tiny Tim's bit earlier shouted out a whoop. Harry heard it and whooped a bit inside himself. He looked again at Shona. He knew she would say the next bit in a way that everyone would find funny.

Dickens: Bob trembled, and got a little nearer to the ruler. He had a momentary idea of knocking Scrooge down with it, holding him, and calling to the people in the court for help and a straitjacket.

Scrooge: A Merry Christmas, Bob! A merrier Christmas, Bob, my good fellow, than I have given you for many a year! I'll raise your salary, and do all I can to assist your struggling family, and we will discuss your affairs this very afternoon, over a Christmas feast, Bob! Make up the fires, and buy another coalscuttle before you dot another *i*, Bob Cratchit.

Dickens: Scrooge was better than his word. He did it all, and infinitely more; and to Tiny Tim, who did not die . . .

Lisa cheered from the back, and it set off a cheer that ran around the auditorium. Shona paused to let it roll before going on.

Dickens: To Tiny Tim, Scrooge was a second father. He became as good a friend, and as good a man, as the good old city knew, or any other good old city, town, or borough, in the good old world.

Some people laughed to see the alteration in him, but he let them laugh, and took little notice of them.

He had no further conversations with Spirits, and it was always said of him, that he knew how to keep Christmas well.

May that be truly said of us, and all of us!
And so, as Tiny Tim observed, God bless
us, every one!

The audience leapt to their feet. They clapped
and cheered and called out, "Merry Christmas,
everyone!"

Lisa looked at Eva and, in the midst of her pride that Harry had done so well, felt a twinge of regret that Ray wasn't there. *Well,* she said to herself, as the cheers slowly subsided around them, *there would be other shows; there would be other Christmases, it's not too late . . . but . . . but . . . even so, if only he had been here this time.*

And as she said that, she saw an expression on Eva's face that seemed so extraordinary and so delighted, it couldn't have been only because of the show—could it? And yet Eva was looking beyond her, behind her.

Lisa turned, and there was Ray.

And at the same time, as Harry and Shona and the cast took their bows, broke the line, and waved to moms, dads, grans and granddads, brothers, sisters, cousins, friends, and teachers, Harry saw that move of Eva's and Mom's, the turn and . . . who was it they were looking at? It was hard to see with the lights still shining in his face . . . Yes, no, yes!

It was Dad. He had come after all. He had seen some of it. He was here, right here at the very moment that people were clapping for him, that Shona was hugging him — OK, embarrassing but nice — and the cast was pushing him to the front of the stage to take a bow all on his own . . . Dad was seeing this too. And he could hear Eva in and among all the cheers and shouts calling out "Harry" in her high voice.

Harry waved and saw quite clearly Dad standing there, doing Dad-clapping. And he saw Mom holding Eva's hand on one side of her and putting her arm around Dad's middle with the other, while he went on and on and on Dad-clapping. *What was that song Mom puts on in the car,* he thought, *something about a "change" . . . wasn't it?*

PARTY
Like a Fezziwig

Use their tips and tricks to make your Christmas the best ever!

Marvelous Mince Pies

The Victorians had the best Christmas snacks! Make sure everyone gets one of these homemade mince pies.

Ingredients

For the filling:
 1 large jar mincemeat (about 22 oz.)
 2 clementines, segmented and diced
 1 apple, grated
 Zest of one lemon

For the pastry:
 2½ cups plain flour
 1¼ cups unsalted butter, softened
 ¾ cup white sugar
 1 large egg

 Confectioners' sugar for topping

Makes 16 mince pies.

Equipment: muffin tin (you may need more than one), mixing bowls, wooden spoon, plastic wrap, rolling pin, round pastry cutter, star-shaped pastry cutter

1. Ask a grown-up to preheat the oven to 400°F and help you butter the muffin tin.
2. Place the flour and butter in a bowl and mix together, using your hands, to a crumb consistency.
3. Add the sugar and the egg, and mix together with the wooden spoon.
4. Pour out onto a lightly floured surface and fold until the pastry comes together.
5. Wrap the pastry in plastic wrap and chill it in the fridge for 10 minutes.
6. Scoop the mincemeat into a bowl and add the clementines, apple, and lemon zest.
7. Roll out the pastry to ⅛ inches.
8. Using a round cutter (about 4 inches), cut out 16 bases and place them into the muffin tin.
9. Put 1½ tablespoons of mincemeat mixture into each.
10. Re-roll out the pastry and cut stars out. Press them on top to seal.
11. Bake mince pies for 15–20 minutes until golden brown.
12. Leave to cool off slightly before releasing them from the muffin tin and dusting with confectioners' sugar.
13. Enjoy!

Make sure you ask an adult to help you.

Parlor Games

No holiday is complete without some games—here are some that were actually played in the nineteenth century!

You're Never Fully Dressed Without a Smile
Pick one person to be "it." That person is the only one in the group who is allowed to smile. They can do anything they want to try and get someone to smile (as long as it does not involve physical contact). If they make someone else smile, that person becomes "it." The last person to smile out of the group is declared the winner.

Pass the Slipper
In Victorian times a shoe would have been used for this game, but any small item may be used.

Pick a player who stands in the center of a circle formed by the other players. The player in the middle must close their eyes, and as they do so, the shoe is passed from player to player behind their back. When the person in the middle opens their eyes, the passing of the shoe immediately stops, and the player must guess who holds the shoe. If they are correct, they change places. Otherwise, the player closes their eyes again and play continues.

Kim's Game
This is a simple memory game, named after Rudyard Kipling's novel *Kim*.

A tray is prepared containing a selection of small articles, preferably unrelated items. Everyone is given a minute to look at the tray and try to remember the contents. The tray is covered or removed, and everyone has to try to make a list of the objects. The person who remembers the most items wins.

Jolly Jokes

Q: Why is it always cold at Christmas?
A: Because it's in Decembrrrrr.

Q: What can you get if you eat Christmas decorations?
A: Tinselitus

Q: Who says "Oh, oh, oh?"
A: Santa Claus walking backwards

Q: Who delivers Christmas presents to cats?
A: Santa Claws

Q: What do you call Santa's little helpers?
A: Subordinate Clauses

Deck the Halls

Deck the halls with boughs of hol-ly! Fa-la-la-l a-la. la la la la
See the blaz-ing yule be-fore us, Fa-la-la-l a-la. la la la la
Fast a-way the old year pass-es, Fa-la-la-l a-la. la la la la

Tis the sea-son to be jol-ly! Fa-la-la-l a-la. la la la la
Strike the harp and join the cho-rus, Fa-la-la-l a-la. la la la la
Hail the new, ye lads and lass-es, Fa-la-la-l a-la. la la la la

Don we now our gay ap-par-el, Fa-la-la-l a-la. la la la la
Fol-low me in mer-ry mea-sure, Fa-la-la-l a-la. la la la la
Sing we joy-ous all to-geth-er, Fa-la-la-l a-la. la la la la

Troll the an-cient Yule-tide car-ol. Fa-la-la-l a-la. la la la la
While I tell of Yule-tide trea-sure, Fa-la-la-l a-la. la la la la
Heed-less of the wind and weath-er, Fa-la-la-l a-la. la la la la

O Christmas Tree

O Christ-mas tree, O Christmas tree, How are thy leaves so
O Christ-mas tree, O Christmas tree, Much plea-sure doth thou
O Christ-mas tree, O Christmas tree, Thy can-dles shine out

ver-dant! O Christ-mas tree, O Christ-mas tree, How
bring me! O Christ-mas tree, O Christ-mas tree, Much
bright - ly! O Christ-mas tree, O Christ-mas tree, Thy

are thy leaves so ver - dant! Not on - ly in the
plea - sure doth thou bring me! For ev - ry year the
can - dles shine out bright - ly! For ev - ry year the

sum - mer - time, But ev'n in win - ter is thy prime. O
Christ - mas tree, Brings to us all both joy and glee, O
Christ - mas tree, Brings to us all both joy and glee, O

Christ-mas tree O, Christ-mas tree, How are thy leaves so ver - dant
Christ-mas tree O, Christ-mas tree, Much plea-sure doth thou bring me!
Christ-mas tree O, Christ-mas tree, Thy can-dles shine out bright- ly!

Jingle Bells

Storytime

It was traditional in Victorian times to tell ghost stories at Christmas. This came from a centuries-old folk custom meant to help pass the long hours of a winter night and to acknowledge, in darkest winter, the death of the old year. This Christmas, gather around the fireplace and tell your own ghost stories, or read this book aloud with your family. You can assign each member a different part.

Merry Christmas, everyone!

About Charles Dickens

Charles Dickens is one of the most famous English writers in history.

Born in Portsmouth, England, in 1812, he is known for works such as *Great Expectations, Oliver Twist,* and *David Copperfield.* In 1843 he wrote *A Christmas Carol,* at a time when Victorians were embracing new Christmas traditions, such as Christmas trees and carol singing.

It was published on December 19, and the first edition sold out by Christmas Eve. Dickens read the book to audiences 127 times in his lifetime—his audiences were old and young, rich and poor, and all related to Dickens's core message of kindness and festive joy.

A Christmas Carol has inspired countless films, TV shows, and retellings—including the one you are holding now.

Michael Rosen

Michael Rosen is one of the best-known figures in the children's book world, renowned for his work as a poet, performer, broadcaster, professor, scriptwriter, and author of classic books such as *We're Going on a Bear Hunt*. He was the British Children's Laureate from 2007 to 2009.

Tony Ross

After training at Liverpool School of Art, Tony Ross worked as a cartoonist, graphic designer, advertising art director, and art lecturer. Today he is best known for the Horrid Henry and Little Princess series of books, as well as illustrating books for David Walliams.

Text copyright © 2017 by Michael Rosen
Illustrations copyright © 2017 by Tony Ross
Party section illustrations by Jason Cox

All rights reserved. No part of this book may be reproduced, transmitted,
or stored in an information retrieval system in any form or by any means,
graphic, electronic, or mechanical, including photocopying, taping,
and recording, without prior written permission from the publisher.

First U.S. edition 2018

Library of Congress Catalog Card Number pending
ISBN 978-1-5362-0479-7

18 19 20 21 22 23 LSC 10 9 8 7 6 5 4 3 2 1

Printed in Crawfordsville, IN, U.S.A.

This book was typeset in Sabon.
The illustrations were done in ink and watercolor.

Walker Books
a division of
Candlewick Press
99 Dover Street
Somerville, Massachusetts 02144

www.walkerbooks.com

FSC
www.fsc.org

MIX
Paper from
responsible sources
FSC® C132124